La Sandra -
Hopefully you enjoy
Book one. Get ready
more twist & turn
Enjoy the read!!

LaSha

Sweeter Than Honey

-written by-

LaTrice Allen

Copyright © 2016 by LaTrice Allen

Published by Bright Beginnings Publications

ISBN 978-0-9862294-8-0

First Edition

Email: snickers0305@gmail.com

Follow on Instagram: @trixntreece

Follow on Twitter: @sydishoney

Cover designer/Graphics: Nicole Mysaysana

Photographer: Ernest Wheeler

Model: Courtne Jones

Editor: Ebony Finley

Proofreaders: Carla Givens, Carla Stevens, La Tanya Harris & Tracey Todd

Acknowledgements

I give God the glory for continuing to keep me grounded. Without Him, I am nothing. I want to thank my fantastic team of proofreaders: Carla Givens, Carla Stevenson, La Tanya Harris & Tracey Todd. Thanks for stepping in and offering to help me, I greatly appreciate you, value your opinions and all the time you put into this project. I love you all! To Ebony Finley, my editor, you are a God-send and I can't thank you enough for all of your help and the love you have shown me. Thank you from the bottom of my heart. The next people I want to thank are: Renee Brown (my sister), Melonee Evans, Glen Banks, Wayne Cooper & Lawrence Dillahunty. You guys helped me so much with developing this story. Thanks for all the calls, brainstorming sessions, comments and suggestions. Without your knowledge, life experiences, and creative minds, I would not have been able to pull this story together. I can't express how valuable you are. I want to thank my daughter, Courtne, for handling my social media, being my cover model, and always there for support and encouragement! I want to thank one of my dearest friends, Helen Wiggins. It seems like every time I go on Facebook, you are publicizing my book. I can't thank you enough for believing in me, our years of friendship and the support you have given me in everything I do. Friends Like you are hard to come by and I thank you so much for being that friend...I love you girl. To my 'bestie circle' (Jane, Shontai, Ced, Troy, Dana, Varick and your significant others) you guys have always had my back for years. Words cannot express how much you all mean to me. Your support is endless and I'm truly grateful for the support and love we have for each other. Last but certainly not least, thank you to all my supporters who sent emails, text messages, Facebook and Instragram messages, or called. Your comments, suggestions, and support, means the world to me! Thank you from the bottom of my heart. P.S. I've already started the last installment of the Honey Series, so it will not take me so long to finish this one...I hope, LOL!

Dedication

I dedicate this book to my baby girl, Courtne. You push me to the limit and you are my biggest supporter. Thank you for always believing in me and having my back! I want to also dedicate this book to all the women who gave their hearts to someone and they didn't know what to do with it. Keep pressing on and don't let one, two, or three bad apples spoil the bunch. The right one is out there and for those we've left behind, thank you for being a part of the big plan...getting us ready for the RIGHT ONE!

Sweeter Than Honey

By

LaTrice Allen

Chapter 1

We have a hostage situation...this is the message that blares across the loud speaker from the negotiator of the Oakland Police Department's S.W.A.T. Team. They are posted in the parking lot of Club Delaney's. The S.W.A.T. team and OPD are on tactical alert. They surround the perimeter of the club; they're in position on the roof and several adjacent buildings, waiting for the word to move in or to fire when the captain gives the command. The Oakland Fire Department, paramedics, and ambulance vehicles are waiting in the parking lot ready to attend to any and all injures that may unfold. This cannot be happening, this looks like something from a T.V. crime show, a movie, or make-believe, because my current situation seems like a bad dream and Lord knows I would just like to wake up from it and all this madness be over. My life has changed for the good and for the bad. Six months ago I met a wonderful man name Phoenix Davenport. Phoenix is my knight in shining armor. Not that I needed one, but he came into my life at the right time. He walked into Club Delaney's and changed my world. In a very short period of time, I met this man and fell madly in love with him. I might add that prior to meeting Mr. Phoenix Davenport, I never knew love existed (outside of my siblings) at least for me, Sydney Denise Marshall. I've protected my heart from being hurt a number of times but sometimes we have no control over things that are meant to be. Now don't get me wrong, Phoenix is not perfect by any means, because no one is, but he's pretty damn close and I'm sure as I get to know him more, I will learn just how perfect he is NOT. However, he's a good man, attentive to my needs, caring, loving, supportive, understanding, compassionate, and the list goes on. We connect on every level. I have never been involved with a man that totally understands me, gets me so to speak and most important of all…does not judge me. He accepts me for who I am, the broken one, and the exotic dancer, which is why this current situation is killing me. With all the drama in my life, past and present, I finally thought all the drama was behind me. Well, I was sadly mistaken because if it were not for bad luck I would not have any luck at all. The drama that constantly follows me is up close and personal once again. "When will the madness stop?" I ask myself through the tears. I say to myself, "Here I go again. As soon as I allow someone in, let my guard down, let go and live a little…it's like Déjàvu…tragedy strikes."

My brother Rocky (not by blood) but my brother from another mother, was left in charge of protecting me while my brother Justin is doing a little time for a stupid mistake he made a few months back. Justin has violent tendencies. He doesn't know how to control his temper and decided to smack his then girlfriend around. Well I guess she got tired of being smacked around, so she called the police and Justin was arrested for domestic violence. Needless to say, she pressed charges and the judge slapped Justin with a one-year jail sentence since this was his first offense. If my brother were here right now, I would not be in this situation. Justin and Rocky have been best friends for years and I have known Rocky for the same amount of time. I love and trust him like he's my true brother. He is also my friend, my dear friend, and one that I trust with my deepest darkest secrets and with my life. Being the star dancer at Club Delaney's comes with a price, a steep price! No one has your back, you can't trust anyone, and everyone is out to get you. But with Rocky by my side, I had nothing to worry about. He was my 'Rock', the one and only (outside of my siblings) I could count on...or so I thought. Never in a million years did I think or even notice that he might have had a 'thing' for me. I noticed he was acting strange on several occasions but he tends to do that when I'm involved with someone. He and my brother always said, "There is no one good enough for you." I should have picked up on the signs, should have been able to tell that he was feeling me on a whole different level. I guess the thought never crossed my mind because again, he was like my brother. So, when Rocky revealed that he loved me and felt like he needed to save me from all the men who were not good for me, it surely took me by surprise. I had just gone through pure hell; I was involved in a hit and run accident where a car ran me over in the parking lot of Kaiser Hospital in San Francisco, which resulted in both of my legs being broken, a medically induced coma due to brain damage, some scrapes and bruises and the horrible memory that will stay with me forever. And to top that off, I found out I'm pregnant with twins...I ask myself, "Could my life be any more screwed up?" I'm still slapping myself for not picking up the signs from Rocky, but there is nothing I can do about it now because he has lost his mind and gone completely crazy. Due to a bad breakup with my ex-boyfriend, Cameron, the cops thought he was the one behind all the threats and was responsible for the hit and run that almost killed me. When Cameron and I split, he could not handle it and tried to kill me one night. Rocky made it to my apartment just in time because if he hadn't, I would not be here to tell this story. Cameron is a bad boy, the star pro football player, and the one with an extremely bad temper. So once he had been arrested for domestic violence, the cops knew Cameron was the lead suspect. Cameron had been trying to apologize for being a total ass and wanted to meet so he could formally apologize to me and move on. At first, I told him to kiss my ass and kick rocks but the detectives in charge of my case convinced me to arrange a meeting at club Delaney's so they could finally catch him. He had been in hiding since the accident, which clearly made him look guilty.

Cameron agreed to meet me at the club on a Friday night at 9:00 pm. The detectives put their plan into action. Phoenix, X (my bodyguard), the detectives, two additional cops and I were the only ones to know of the plan. They indicated the less people who knew of the plan, the less likely our plan would be blown. I felt bad because I knew Rocky should have been a part of this master plan, but I was advised against it. So we set the plan in motion. Phoenix, X and myself arrive at the club at 7:00pm to prepare for the night. Once we pull into the parking lot of the club, Ben, Phoenix's driver, pulls his Lincoln Towne car into our designated parking stall next to the entrance. Ben exits the driver's side and opens the trunk to retrieve my wheelchair. By this time, X has exited the passenger front seat and opens the back door for Phoenix to exit. He exits and leans in to help me out the car. I gently place my arm around his neck and he lifts me up and gently places me in the wheelchair. X is at the entrance talking to Rocky. Phoenix bends down, leans close to my ear and whispers,

"Are you ready baby?" I nod yes, when in fact, I'm not. I'm scared as hell and pray to God that all goes according to plan. He then tells me that everything will be okay because he and X will be inside the club. Phoenix kisses me on the lips and proceeds to push me towards the entrance. When it all goes down, at least I will be protected by law enforcement inside and outside the club. There will be no way for Cameron to escape. Once I roll through the entrance of the club, Rocky bends down to give me a kiss. I turn my face to give him access to my cheek but he turns my face and kisses me in the mouth. I have so much other stuff on my mind right now that I dismiss what he has just done and tell myself I will address the kiss later with him. Rocky has an evil smirk on his face but again I dismiss, my focus was what lies ahead of us. Phoenix pushes me through the club until I spot my girl CoCo. He leaves me to catch up with CoCo and returns to converse with X. Outside of the disrespectful kiss and the evil grin he displayed on his face, Rocky is back to business as usual, chatting with some of the club's staff members and preparing for the club's opening. The doors are scheduled to open at 8:00 pm as they do every day except Sundays. So we will see just how normal this evening will really get once Cameron brings his crazy ass up in here. Rocky was unaware of what was going down, or so I thought. I told him that Cameron was coming to personally apologize for being the biggest jerk in the world. I'd ask him not to give Cameron a hard time so I could get his apology and move on with my life...and hopefully he would do the same. Rocky's facial expression showed me that he was not too happy with my request but indicated he would do as I asked so I could put that relationship behind me. Cameron had agreed to meet me at the club at 9:00 pm, but he was late. It was now after 10:00 pm and he still has not shown up. I decide to go into Delaney's office to do some paperwork and get my mind off the fact that the crazy man Cameron will be a no-show. I slowly roll the wheelchair towards the back of the club, where Delaney's office is. As I roll pass the bar at the rear of the club, I slightly acknowledge the undercover cops at the bar with a glance, they both nod with acknowledgement.

Once in the office, I close and lock the office door. I make my way over to the desk and push myself out of the wheelchair and into the high-back black leather chair that's planted behind the large oak desk. Once settled in the chair, I retrieve my cell phone from my pocket and text Phoenix. "I guess he's not coming babe. I'm going to complete some paperwork. Let me know if the detective calls off the plan or if he decides to show." I hit the send button and sit my cell phone on top of the oak desk. I really just wanted to go home and get off my feet because I was tired and completely stressed out. Seconds later my cell phone dinged, indicating I received a text message. I reach for my phone, slid my middle finger across the bottom, entered my secret code and hit the text message icon with the #1 in the upper right corner. Phoenix had replied to my text message. "We will wait until 11:00 babe and if Cameron doesn't show, we will pack it up and call it a night. I love you and everything will work out...don't worry." I told him that was easy for him to say. I proceeded to complete the paperwork in front of me on the cluttered oak desk. Fifteen minutes later I hear what sounds like gunshots. I jump in the chair as I was startled by the shots. My heart starts to race, as I was not sure what is going on on the other side of the office door. I glance over to the door to make sure I had indeed locked it behind me. I did. I breathe a slight sigh of relief then frantically start to open and close each of the desk drawers, not sure what I was looking for or what I would find but I would know if I found it. The last drawer on the right was locked. I go back to the top drawer in the middle of the desk that was just above my knees. I slightly push back the high-back black leather executive chair so I can gain full access of the drawer and its contents. When I open the drawer again, it housed general office supplies…pens, paperclips, staples, glue sticks, and a key ring with 2 small keys attached. I take the keys from the drawer and try the first of the two keys…it doesn't work. I then try the second key and thank God it works. Once inside, I notice there is a gun. A shiny semi-22 automatic with a white pearl handle sat at the bottom of the drawer with a small box of bullets next to it. I removed the gun and the box of bullets and placed them on top of the desk. I quickly fiddle around with it; being extremely careful in case it was loaded. I surely didn't want to accidently shoot myself. I managed to open the chamber and luckily it was empty. I removed one bullet at a time from the box of bullets and placed one in each of the chambers holes. Once it is full, I snap the chamber back into place. I then gently place the gun back on the top of the desk right in front of me. My right hand lie next to the gun shaking, but ready to grab and shoot if need be. I haven't shot a gun since I was a kid, hunting with my father and uncles. I'm sure it will all come back to me…point and shoot…at any signs of danger.

Suddenly there was then an awkward silence. I picked up my iPhone and placed my thumb on the button, which identifies my fingerprint to open the phone for use. I sent a text to Phoenix and Rocky to see what is going on. I get no response. A million thoughts were racing through my head. "Is everyone okay? Did anyone get shot? Did Cameron eventually show up?" I had no answers to my questions. It feels like an eternity and I am disconnected from the outside world. I look at my cell phone and it has only been two minutes since I texted Phoenix and Rocky, still with no reply so I text them both again. I'm even more scared at this point because I have not gotten a response from either one of them. "My God, what's going on out there," I ask myself. Finally my cell phone dings with a text message. "Oh thank God," I say when I realize the text is from Rocky. I'm relieved when I read that Rocky indicates everything is okay and that the situation was under control and it is safe for me to come out.

I place the gun back in the bottom right-hand drawer and cover it with papers. I lock it and place the keys in my pocket. I exhaled and thanked God that all is well. I pull my wheelchair closer and position myself in it. I place my right hand on the right wheel and my left hand on the left wheel and move in the direction of the door. Once there, I unlock it and wheel myself out. As I make my way to the main room of the club I think that it's too quiet. I have a bad feeling, something's not right, I think to myself. I reach the main room of the club and my worst nightmare comes to life...the plan of the detectives has gone completely wrong. I look to the left and see that both undercover cops are on the floor with their guns in their hands and blood spilling from multiple bullet holes in their bodies. I gag and almost vomit at the sight. I then see my best friend CoCo; she slightly sticks her head from behind the bar. We make eye contact and she nods letting me know she's ok. I look to the right and see that X has also been shot and is not moving, even though he was a pain in my ass I didn't want anything to happen to him and my heart sunk. This is horrible. I cautiously moved through the club seeing some of the club goers on the floor hurt and other just taking cover not knowing what else to do. I guess the majority of the other club goers made it out of the club safe when all the mayhem started. I saw Rocky pacing the floor and sweating profusely, like an insane mad man. Rocky stops pacing and looks in my direction with an evil look on his face. As I move closer, my heart sinks to my stomach, Phoenix and Cameron are on their knees with their hands tied behind their backs. Rocky looks disturbed and moves behind them pointing the gun at the back of their heads. I finally swallow the lump in my throat so that I could speak. "Rocky, what is going on here? Why do you have them tied up and on their knees with a gun to their heads? What the hell is wrong with you? Are you on drugs? Have you lost your everlasting mind?" I shout! With a disturbed look, he stares at me and the look on his face scares the hell out of me. I have never seen Rocky like this before...it's like he's possessed. I'm not sure what has happened to him but he has apparently had some type of psychotic break. "Rocky, what is going on?" I ask again, but in a much softer, more caring tone. He moves from behind Phoenix and Cameron and slowly walks over to me. He stops inches away from my face, places both hands on either side, draws me closer and kisses me, not with an open mouth but lips to lips. He holds the kiss for what seems like forever, breathing heavy, then pulls away from my lips and slowly speaks in a raspy tone, "Getting rid of the problem...I mean, the problems that are keeping us apart." "What do you mean keeping us apart?" I respond. Rocky looks at me with this blank expression on his face and yells, "Sydney, you cannot be this stupid!" I jump as his voice echoes throughout the club and pierce my eardrums. Did this asshole just call me stupid, I think to myself? Now I'm not only scared but I'm pissed at the fact the he has clearly lost his mind and at this point I have to 'match' his crazy. I yell back, "What the hell are you talking about?" "Don't you fucking raise your voice at me! You are not the star of this show tonight, I am. So sit your ass down and let me handle my business. You, your 'Rich Boy' and the cops thought you were going to keep me out of the loop. But I showed you, I showed you all that you can't keep anything from Rocky! I knew at some point your asshole 'Rich Boy' boyfriend was going to remove me from the equation so, I had to be prepared for when he did and thought of my own little master plan. First, I planted a bug and a tracking device in your duffle bag, because you never go anywhere without it. I hired three knuckleheads from Richmond with nothing to lose and paid them five hundred dollars each to come to the club, strapped and ready to shoot on my command," Rocky explains. Rocky and his goons shot my bodyguard X, the undercover cops, and anyone else who got in their way. I was dumbfounded and in complete shock! Rocky obviously had a plan and he waited for the right time to execute that plan...a plan all his own...a plan that has Phoenix,

Cameron, and myself in this crazy situation at this very moment and a number of people either hurt or dead.

Chapter 2

Tears are rolling down my face. I look at Rocky with as much compassion as I can muster up at that moment and tell him that I do love him. I've always loved him but as a brother and nothing else. I express that this is crazy and if he doesn't let everyone go he could end up hurt or dead. "Well that's the price I will have to pay," he responds. "It doesn't have to be; please let them go," I plead. At that moment, CoCo came from behind the bar and made a noise that made Rocky turn in her direction, pointing his gun and ready to shoot if need be. CoCo raises her hands high in the air and over her head and says, "It's me Rocky, please don't shoot!" Rocky shows a sign of relief and says, "Girl you almost got yourself killed up in here. Bring your ass from behind that damn bar." CoCo did as she was told and walked slowly in my direction, sat in a chair next to me and grabbed my hand. Tears were streaming down her face and she is shaking like a leaf. I squeeze her hand and try to give her some comfort that I am there. Even though I have no idea how this whole situation is going to play out. I knew deep inside it was not going to end well. I knew at this moment there would be more bloodshed and more lives lost. The million-dollar question was, whose blood would be shed and who would lose their life. CoCo whispered, "Why is he doing this Syd?" I shake my head indicating that I don't know. Rocky spins around and yells, "You bitches better be quiet, I need to think."

The phone inside the club located near the DJ booth rang and startled all of us. Rocky laughs and says, "I wonder who that is?" He walks over to the DJ booth and picks up the ringing phone. "Yeah, what's up," he answers. "That's going to be hard to do my man," he says into the receiver of the phone. What's going to be hard to do, I think. Then Rocky continues to talk to whoever is on the other end. "Look here, this is how this shit is going to play out. I need for y'all to have that driver Ben to back up the car as close to the front entrance as he can, then me and these two assholes, Phoenix and Cameron gone come out, get into the car and ride off into the sunset." He's laughing and who knows what because no one else can hear the conversation. Rocky hangs up the phone and walks over to me and CoCo. He looks at me, smiles, then at CoCo and says, "CoCo, you cool as hell. So sorry you had to get caught up in this mess. I don't have beef with you, I'm gonna let you go." He looks around the room and says, "Anybody else up in here that ain't hurt, y'all can leave too." Nobody moves. "What the fuck y'all fools waiting for. A written invitation? I said get the hell out of here before I change my mind!" he screams. At that moment, several people who were slightly injured and those who weren't injured at all made a beeline for the front entrance. CoCo tightens her grip and looks at me still with tears streaming from her eyes and speaks, "I can't leave you Syd." I smile and tell her I will be okay and she needs to go. I could tell she really didn't want to leave my side. Trust me, I appreciate her effort but I squeezed her hand and whispered, "You have to go babe; you got two babies to be there for. Now get your ass up and get the hell out of here." CoCo stands, hugs me, kisses me on the cheek and tells me she loves me and that she will see me soon. With that, she heads towards the front entrance then stops and turns back to me and says, "Sydney, I can't leave you!" Rocky screams, "You stupid bitch, you should have left when I gave you the chance!" He lifts his right hand that's holding the gun, aims it in her direction and fires twice. I scream as I watch in horror my best friend's lifeless body drop to the floor.

I start to wheel myself in the direction of CoCo, as my movement is cloudy from all the tears that are falling from my eyes. It's like a rainstorm, a torrential downpour of tears exiting from my tear ducts; the faster I wipe them away the more they come. Rocky grabs the handle on the back of the wheelchair and asks, "Who's next? Since you fools don't think I'm serious." I scream, "Let me go, you sick son of a bitch! CoCo has done nothing to you, you bastard! She has two kids and you have just taken their mother. You are going to rot in hell!" With all of his might, he grips the handle of the wheelchair once again but this time he lifts it, knocking me to the floor. I look back at Rocky and say, "I swear, I will kill you myself." Rocky displays this evil smirk on his face, he walks around the wheelchair and kicks me in the stomach, saying, "You'll have to catch me first bitch." I'm doubled over in pain. I hold my stomach while rocking back and forth to try to ease the pain, and pray that my babies are fine. Phoenix calls out for me. Rocky has snapped and the demons have taken over his body, like the Invasion of the Body Snatchers (an old movie) from back in the day. Rocky sits the wheelchair up, picks me up and places me back in the wheelchair. He tells me to sit down and not say another word. He looks at me with some compassion and whispers, "I don't like to hurt you, so please don't make me do it again. CoCo left me no choice, I had to kill her babe, please understand." At that moment, all the anger rose up in me again and with all my might, I raised my right hand and slapped Rocky across his face as hard as I could. He stood there for a second, staring at me with steam coming from his ears, and says through clenched teeth, "I'll give you that one babe, you're upset about your girl, I get it…but if you ever put your fucking hands on me again, I will rip your heart out with my bare hands!" The look that Rocky gave me made me believe there would be no doubt in my mind that he would do as he said. The phone rings again breaking his cold stare. He rolls his eyes at me then walks over to the DJ booth and answers the phone. "WHAT!" he screams into the receiver. He's quiet for a moment, obviously listening to what's being said on the other end. "Those shots were for CoCo. I gave her the opportunity to leave. She chose to stay, so she had to go. I'm sorry about CoCo. She was not a part of the big plan. But sometimes the plan needs to be altered. Please know that if I peek out of this door and Ben is not in front of the entrance with the car, someone else will die, now make this shit happen!" Rocky yells and hangs up the phone. He walks over to Phoenix and Cameron and tells them he doesn't know why the cops think he's bullshitting and that he won't hesitate to pump some more lead inside the bodies still in the club. Cameron starts to sob. Rocky looks at him like he is crazy and laughs. "I see mister tough guy is a bitch after all. Shut yo crying ass up!" he yells, then strikes Cameron across the head with the butt of the gun.

Thank goodness Rocky's rant is interrupted by the sound of a car horn on the other side of the club's door. He walks over to the door, slightly cracks it and peeks through. Rocky sees that Ben has pulled the car as close to the door as he can without blocking its entrance. Rocky walks over to me and says, "I'll be back for you baby. I need to get rid of some of this dead weight first." I begin to cry once more and try to plead with him not to do this and to let Phoenix and Cameron go. I grab his arm to stop him from moving closer to Phoenix and Cameron but my efforts go unwarranted. I'm no match for him. I wheel myself over to Phoenix as quickly as I can. I bend down easing myself out of the chair and in front of him and place my hands on each side of his face and kiss him passionately. I whisper in his ear, "I'm so sorry all this is happening and I love you very much. Everything is going to be okay; they will not let Rocky get away with this." He looks at me with the deepest compassion and tells me, "You are my life Sydney Marshall. I've waited all my life for someone like you and now that you are in my life and carrying our babies, I'm not going anywhere. I'll be alright! I need for you to be strong baby for the twins and me. Can you do that for me?" he asks. I shake my head yes and our lips meet once again, then our tears meet on our cheeks as I hold him close to me. My heart is breaking into a million pieces. The thought of not having Phoenix in my life is killing me. Rocky yells for me to let him go and I hug him tighter. Phoenix tells me "it's okay baby" and before he can say another word, I release my tight hold on him and grab my right side as a sharp pain shoots through my side. Rocky has kicked me once again. "I said move bitch!" he screams while looking down at me with a smirk on his face. I'm still holding my side in pain while looking at him when he draws his right leg back like he's getting ready to kick a football for the field goal and with all of his might, kicks me in the stomach, this time knocking the wind out of me. I get dizzy, unable to breathe and feel like I am about to pass out from the amount of pain my body is experiencing at this very moment. Phoenix yells and says, "If it's the last thing I do, I will kill you for hurting her, you sorry piece of shit!" Rocky laughs, "Good luck with that man," he replies. Rocky stands behind Cameron and pulls him to his feet then does the same with Phoenix. He ushers them both to the front of the club and once again peeks out the front door to see if Ben is still out front. Rocky confirmed Ben was still waiting; he turns to Phoenix and Cameron and says, "This is how this is going to play out. I will open the door and both of you will step out side by side. I will be behind you both using you as my human shield. We will all get into the back seat of the car. If either of you try anything other than what I have just instructed, I will blow your fucking brains out right where you stand. Do I make myself clear?" They both nod in agreement. Rocky slowly pushes the door open and all three proceed out the doors with his plan in motion. A few seconds later, I hear the tires screech and the car speed away. Little did I know, they would not get far.

I try and use all the strength that I have to get up off the floor and into my wheelchair. The pain I feel is far too much for me to bear. Seconds later, the doors of the club's entrance fling open and I see what the club looks like as an army of cops swarm in. Someone finds the main light switch, turns it on and brings light to a dark situation. Orders are being barked all around me. I hear someone say that one of the undercover cops was still alive and the other one was gone. I heard someone yell to get the medics inside because they had a few more survivors. The detectives rush over to me with medics on their heels. They quickly assess me, and begin to help me onto a gurney. I refuse and ask to be seated in my wheelchair. "He shot CoCo," I say in a weak voice. The detective informs me that they have her and she is still alive, barely but still alive and is being rushed to the hospital. I thank God for saving CoCo and pray that He does the same for Phoenix, Ben and Cameron. I miraculously get the strength of an ox and hop out of the wheelchair, hobbling towards the door screaming, "Where's Phoenix!?" The detectives are right by my side helping me to the door. Once outside, the club is surrounded by T.V. networks, SWAT vans, police cars, and more ambulances. The car that has Ben in the driver's seat did not get very far as he is barricaded in the parking lot not able to escape. The commander comes on the loud speaker instructing Rocky to give himself up and let the hostages go. This situation would make a good book; Cameron, the man I had a relationship with but never loved, the man I fell in love with just a few short months ago and the man I call my brother, their lives are all hanging in the balance not knowing who will survive this situation and who will perish.

So here we are now, Rocky is not responding to the commander. The police are speaking in codes and I'm not sure what is going to happen and I am scared. I face Detective Watson and plead with him that there is no more

24

bloodshed. "I can't promise you that Ms. Marshall, but we will do our best," he responds. "There's movement!" one of the cops announces over the loud speaker. The back passenger window slowly comes down and the commander yells, "Hold your fire." Rocky then screams, "I love you Sydney, this is all for us!" The commander gets on the loud speaker and tells Rocky this is his final warning, and that he better come out with his hands up or they will come in to get him. He indicates he will count to three and if he doesn't come out, they're coming in. The commander counts to three and still no response from Rocky. He tells one of the officers that he wants to hit the car with tear gas and the officer nods in agreement. I turn to the commander and ask, "Won't the tear gas harm them and can't they get hurt by the broken glass?" He gives me a sympathetic look and says, "The goal is to de-escalate the situation. The tear gas will burn their eyes and might cause nausea. The glass will not break when we shoot it in the back window, it will make a hole in the glass but the entire glass will not shatter." This information calms my nerves just a bit but not enough for me to be assured that the situation is completely under control. All of a sudden, the unthinkable happens, and my heart stops beating. There were shots fired, four to be exact and muzzle flashes were seen from within the car. The officer next to me yells, "Shots fired, move in with the tear gas...now!" The commander says as he now is pacing and holding his head. I'm holding my breath waiting to see what happens next. When the cop shoots the tear gas, I hear the whistling sound and look up to see a hole in the back rear window with a thick smoke seeping from it. Everyone around me seems to be moving in slow motion, like bees swarming around something sweeter than honey. The SWAT team and the Oakland PD are waiting for the command to move in. The commander comes on the loud speaker and says, "Rocky, what's going on? Is anyone hurt?" There is no response or movement from inside the car. "What the hell is going on? Somebody tell me what's happening!" I scream. My heart is beating a mile a minute and I'm screaming to no one in particular, "Why is this happening!?" I am hoping someone, anyone, will give me a logical explanation as to why I am living this nightmare. The commander speaks in his walkie-talkie, which comes through the speakers of the ground officers surrounding the perimeter. He tells them to take their position and be ready to move on his command. The officers are scrambling around with precision, positioning themselves to make their move. "Why is this taking so long? Why haven't they got to the car yet? Is everyone still alive or are they all dead?" These are the questions I'm asking myself because no one is answering my questions. Yeah, I guess they are a little busy at the moment but I need answers and I need them now!

The commander gives the officers the go-ahead to move in. There are now eight officers in position at the car. Two are at the front of the vehicle, two on each side of the passenger and front doors, and two at the rear of the car, all with rifles drawn and ready to shoot if need be. This is not to mention the magnitude of the other officers and SWAT that are still in position around the parameter. By this time there is very little smoke from the tear gas seeping from the back window. It is still difficult to see what the situation is inside the vehicle due to the dark limousine tint that covers all windows. One of the officers moves slowly to the front driver's front door with caution. His partner is close by his side with his rifle pointed at the window. The first officer reaches his hand out and places it on the door handle to open the door. He tugs at the handle but the door remains closed. He then cautiously moves to the driver's side back door and tries to open it as well. The officer motions for them to fall back. Once they are back in position, one of the officers motions for the officers on the other side of the vehicle to try the doors on the passenger side. The officers on the opposite side of the vehicle repeat the movements of the first cops and found that those doors are locked as well. Once they were back in position, the lead officer reports on his microphone that is attached to his left shoulder of his uniform shirt that all doors are locked. With no response, the commander gets on the loud speaker one last time and demands that Rocky give himself up and exit the vehicle with his hands up. Once again, there is no response or movement in the vehicle. You can hear a pin drop in the area as everyone holds their breath waiting to see if Rocky will give himself up. I, on the other hand, have a very bad feeling and fear the worst. Rocky has truly lost his mind. He thought by killing Phoenix, Cameron and Ben that he will have me all to himself. I know I sound like a broken record but for the life of me I cannot understand why this is happening; and I can't comprehend why I didn't see the signs that Rocky has obviously been writing on the walls in bright red letters. I am truly off my game. But who would have thought in a million years that this scene would be playing out like it is at this very moment with my best friend, my brother, Rocky as the big bad monster in a horror movie.

Chapter 3

After the commander gives the order to move in, the lead officer on the driver's side moves in slowly, still with his rifle drawn and approaches the vehicle once again. He knows that the doors are locked but double checks to make sure. He then moves to the back door on the same side of the vehicle and double checks it as well. The officer motions for one of the cops on the opposite side of the vehicle to try the doors on the passenger side. The officer does and confirms that those doors are locked too. The lead officer pulls his baton off of his hip and in one quick move his baton expands. He moves closer to the driver's side of the vehicle and before I can blink, the window is shattered. As this is being done, the other officer is right next to him on his right side with his rifle drawn and ready to shoot if need be. There is no movement and everyone is holding their breath waiting to see what will happen. The officer then reaches inside the car and unlocks the doors. He motions for the other officers to stand back as he opens the driver's side door. As I watch all of this unfold, everyone appears to be moving in slow motion when in reality they are moving pretty swiftly, but very carefully. As the driver's side door opens, Ben's motionless body slumps out of the driver's seat and onto the asphalt. The officer moves in and applies two fingers to Ben's neck to see if he has a pulse. He reaches for his mic and informs all that he's alive and to send a 'bus' over, that's "ambulance" in cop terminology. I breathe a sigh of relief but my heart is still pounding waiting on the outcome of the other three in the car. An officer standing next to me says, "One down and three to go, I pray they are all alive." "You and me both," I

29

reply. The ambulance that is at the front of the line reaches them within seconds. Both medics jump out at the same time. One quickly rushes over to tend to Ben while the other is pulling a gurney with a third medic who is in the back of the ambulance. They place him on the gurney and quickly move him away from the vehicle so they can assess his injuries. While they are taking his vitals and preparing to transport him to the closest hospital, I turn to Detective Watson and inquire where they are taking him. "Highland General Hospital," he responds. "Highland General Hospital?" I question. "That is a county hospital and both Ben and Phoenix have medical insurance. Why are they taking them to Highland and not Summit?" I ask. Detective Watson confirms that Highland General Hospital is a county hospital but they are better prepared for trauma cases than the other neighboring hospitals. "My God, that's where they take drive-by victims and gunshot victims," I whisper. But not low enough because Detective Watson looks at me and says, "Exactly! They will be in good hands so let's just stay positive. Ok?" "Okay," I reply. I hold my head down for a moment because I feel like I have just been chastised by my father for being ungrateful. That was a brief moment because something comes over me and I then yell, "What are you people waiting for? Why is this taking so long?" The detective turns, looks at me with an irritating expression and replies, "We have to completely neutralize the situation before we can proceed. We are doing our best under the circumstances, please be patient and let us do our job." "If you were doing your damn job, we would not be in this situation right now, now would we?" I snap. The detective looks at me again for a moment then turns his attention back to the matter at hand. It's clear that I'm upset and I know that these people are doing their best to get control of this situation, and bring this madness to an end.

The officer is now at the back door on the driver's side. Once the door is open, there was a clear view of the unthinkable. There lay Cameron, Phoenix, and Rocky all slumped over each other with an abundance of blood everywhere. Now that I think about it, I didn't remember seeing any visible blood on Ben when they removed him from the car, I thought. It really doesn't matter because what I'm seeing right now has me about to pass out. The officer reports on the mic that, "We have three down." He informs the commander there is still no movement and he is going in." The commander gives the order for him to proceed with caution. The officer steps slightly in the back then quickly out. He reports that Rocky is holding a gun and that he will move back in to retrieve it. The officers did just that. He slowly moves in and gets the gun out of Rocky's hand. He hands it to another officer who places it in a plastic bag. The officer then tells a fellow officer on the opposite side of the vehicle that it will be better to remove Rocky from that side. All officers move into their positions to retrieve Rocky's body from the backseat. Once they remove Rocky, the lead officer reports that it's visible that he suffered a self-inflicted wound under his chin from his position in the vehicle and how he was holding the gun. He checks for a pulse, indicates he has a strong one and requests a bus. Within seconds, another ambulance appears and follows the same procedure as they did for Ben. Next out the backseat was Cameron. The officer checks for a pulse and reports that Cameron is shot in the chest and he is unable to find a pulse. He still has to follow protocol, which requires him to follow the same routine as the others and call for a bus. My heart is on the outside of my chest and it's so heavy right now. Even though Cameron was indeed a hothead, crazy, and even tried to kill me, I don't want him dead. We did have some fun times and I will just have to remember those times. Once this nightmare is over, I will put it as far out of my mind as possible. I watch them cover his body with a white sheet and take him away. I literally cannot breath. I'm trying to catch my breath and keep my composure at the same time. Here's that slow motion movement again. I feel like I'm watching a Spike Lee movie where the people move slowly and appear to be floating through the air. I take a deep breath again then exhale and wait for the report from the officer on the man I have fallen madly in love with and the father of my unborn children. It feels like it's taking him forever to update the commander on his findings. What is taking so damn long, I wonder? I dare not ask the detective for fear that he just might shoot me to keep me quiet! The officer finally removes Phoenix from the backseat and his entire lifeless body is covered in blood. The officer repeats procedure by checking for a pulse. He then reports that Phoenix has been shot in the neck and there is a faint pulse. Before he can request the bus, it was pulling alongside the vehicle. I turn to Detective Watson and beg with pleading eyes that he allow me to ride with Phoenix in the ambulance to the hospital. The detective and commander both give me a look of compassion and both agree that it is okay for me to accompany him. Detective Watson releases the brakes on the wheelchair; they both proceed to wheel me in the direction of the ambulance at a very fast pace. The commander tells the lead officer to let the medics know that I am coming along. We approach the ambulance and I begin to feel weak. The detective locks the wheels and he and the commander help me to stand, interlocking my arms with theirs.

As I look around at the 'crime scene', I become nauseous and feel the need to throw up. All the blood and mayhem plus the fact that Phoenix is near death have finally taken a toll on me. The thought of losing him has literally got me sick to my stomach. We are moving close to the ambulance and I stop in my tracks, lean over and let out what I could no longer keep in. The commander moves to the left, trying not to get stomach contents all over his shoes. However, the detective didn't move. In fact, he moves my hair back, rubs my back in a circular comforting motion and says, "That's it sweetheart. Let it all out. You'll feel better once you have emptied your stomach. This is no place for you to be and all of this is way too much to handle. With the events of this day and how the plan failed, I am so sorry for that and please know Sydney that if we knew things would have turned out like this we would have never involved you, Phoenix or Ben." His voice got deep and almost to a whisper, I can tell he is struggling with his words. The detective reaches in his upper left pocket of his black suit jacket and hands me a handkerchief. I stand up straight, holding my stomach and reach for the handkerchief to wipe my mouth. Detective Watson stares at me for a moment, then says, "Sydney, I am so very sorry for the chain of events that have unfolded today. I'm angry that Phoenix and Ben are injured and I'm praying for their speedy recoveries. I never wanted Cameron to get hurt let alone killed, and I'm still in a state of shock at how wrong we were about everything." I look at the detective and I'm just as angry if not more and I'd like to punch him in the face for putting all of us in this situation. But, I can't because we all agreed to execute the plan and I more than anyone wanted Cameron arrested. How could anyone know Rocky was on to us and created a master plan of his own, one that he set out to remove every man from my life? So far he was successful at doing just that. There is a loud horn that brought us back from our unspoken stares, the sirens start to blare bringing an urgent melody to the parking lot letting us know that we need to hurry and get to the ambulance so they can get Phoenix to the emergency room. With tears forming in the detective's eyes, he grabs my hand and we continue our walk towards the ambulance. We reach the back of the ambulance and the medic extends a hand for me to grab. Detective Watson lends another hand and with the help of them both, I am lifted up and into the back of the ambulance. The detective steps back to allow the medic to close the doors. Before the doors close, he tells me that he will meet me at the hospital. There are two medics in the back of the ambulance and one instructs me to sit in a chair that is off to the side and away from them and their patient. The medic says with a smile, "Ma'am, we need for you to strap yourself in as we will be traveling at a high speed and can make some sudden stops in the process. We have enough to worry about with your husband here and will be focusing on keeping him stable; we don't need for you to get hurt as well. I know this will be hard to do but please try to relax and we will be pulling up to Highland General's Emergency Room within six minutes." I say to myself, "This is going to be the longest six minutes of our lives." I try to form a smile but somehow my lips will not move in an upward position so I nod my head up and down to acknowledge his request. No one is saying anything. The only talking are all the machines that are beeping in their own language letting the medics know that they are doing their job. Both medics are moving about. One is looking at the monitors, and writing down the readings, the other is preparing a medication of some sort in a syringe. I want to ask what it is but again I can't form my lips to speak this time. I have never been so scared in my life. My heart is broken as I look at Phoenix lying on the stretcher. He has a thick bandage wrapped around his neck; I imagine this is to control the bleeding that is coming from the gunshot wound to his neck. There's blood everywhere, which is making me sick again. I swallow to try and keep what's left in my stomach down. "Just turn away," I tell myself but I can't stop staring at the man I'm madly in love with and plus I want to make a mental note as to all they are doing to him. He has a peaceful look about him, likes he's resting or sleeping. I don't want him to rest or sleep right now. I want him to open his eyes, turn to me and tell me he will be okay. Somehow this horrible feeling in my stomach is making me think otherwise, despite being optimistic. Phoenix has an IV running from his left arm pumping fluids into his veins. The blood pressure machine is inflating on its own, reading his blood pressure and heart rate, which reads 70/51 with a heart rate of 40. My goodness that's low, I think. As soon as the numbers appear on the monitor, the medic makes notes of the numbers.

I want to get close to Phoenix, touch him, and let him know I'm here with him. I think about asking the medic if I can move closer but remember I didn't find my voice earlier so I just sit there listening and watching. I heard a voice come over the ambulance intercom, "Station 52 come in." The driver picks up his receiver and responds, "Station 52, go ahead." "This is Dr. Castleberry at Highland General and we need your ETA," he said. "We're two minutes out," the driver responds. "Okay, just checking. It's a mad house over here. We have four DOA's (dead on arrival), four gunshot patients already headed to surgery and waiting for the last one to arrive. We need an update on the patient," the doctor requests. The driver gives the doctor a quick overview of Phoenix's status and informs him they are almost there. I take this opportunity to make my move and take my chances of getting closer to Phoenix. I unlock my belt and slowly move closer to Phoenix. The medic turns and gives me a stern look but his look softens a bit when he sees the look of disparity on my face. He gave me permission to move close to Phoenix. I lean in close to Phoenix, grab his bloody hand and whisper in his ear, "Baby, it's Sydney. I need you to pull through this. You promised me you would always be there for me, for us, so you better not leave me, you better not leave us! We need you, Auntie Hattie needs you and your best friend needs you. Baby, Ben is still alive, so you see, you can't leave us. I love you so much, you are my life and we bring joy to each other. You're my hero, my best friend, my lover and the father of our babies." All of a sudden my conversation is cut short when one of the monitors starts beeping, not the beep pause, beep pause rhythm but a long beeping sound. The medic close to me pushes me out of the way and shouts, "We're losing him!" I back up in the corner, pull my knees to my chest and start rocking back and forth. I cover my mouth to muffle my screams as the tears stream down my face like a rapid river.

Chapter 4

"Clear," the medic shouts as he holds the defibrillator on Phoenix's chest and proceeds to shock his heart. Phoenix's chest lifts off the stretcher and both medics look at the monitor and wait for a reading that indicates his heart is beating again. The medic shouts again, "Clear!" He repeats the process again still with no reading from the monitor. "One more time!" he shouts. "He's gone," the other medic says. "No! Do it again! You keep doing it until his heart starts again, do you hear me!? Do it again and don't you stop!" I scream to the top of my lungs. "I'm sorry ma'am but he's gone," he says with sympathy in his voice and in his eyes. "Please no! I beg you, you have to save him! Please shock him again, please don't give up on him! He's a strong man, he can handle it, shock him again!" I plead as I drop to the floor. I quickly crawl over to Phoenix and shout, "Don't you fucking leave me Phoenix! Do you hear me!? Rocky survived, do you want him to still have control and possibly hurt me again, hurt our babies? I'll answer for you...No, I don't think so, then you better get that damn heart of yours beating or I will kill you myself!" I am so angry and scared all at the same time but I had to do something, say something and hopefully he hears my little pep talk and turns this situation around. I'm hoping he heard how much I love him moments ago but when one is faced with an emotional situation, there is no way of monitoring or controlling what comes from their mouth. In all of the commotion, I didn't even realize the ambulance has stopped moving and suddenly the back doors fly open. The medic holding the defibrillator hands it to the other medic and tells him, "I have to try and save this man."

They pull the stretcher out of the ambulance and the medic then jumps on the stretcher and straddles Phoenix to begin chest compressions. There are a number of people outside the ambulance moving and rushing to get the situation under control. I'm on the floor and the other medic reaches down to help me up and out of the ambulance. He tells me he's very sorry and before I know it, I take my right hand and slap him as hard as I can across his face. Through clenched teeth I reply, "You gave up on him and if he dies, you will share the blame in his death and his blood will also be on your hands." There is a hospital guard standing near the entrance of the ER, he sees what has just transpired and brings over a wheelchair and asks that I sit down. The medic doesn't say a word; he just looks at me while holding the side of his face. Immediately after Phoenix is removed from the ambulance, a nurse helps the medic out by placing a balloon-like contraption with a mouthpiece over Phoenix's mouth, squeezes and counts to three. Once she stops counting, the medic proceeds with chest compressions. The security guard is wheeling me right behind them. I continue to pray that God allows his heart to start beating again. We reach an elevator and within a second, the door opens; two doctors, two nurses, the guard, medic, the Phoenix and myself all pile inside. One of the doctors tells the guard to hit the 5th floor. The guard follows the instructions. Everyone inside the evaluator is quiet until the medic shouts, "I got a pulse! It's weak, but I got a pulse!" Everyone looks in the direction of Phoenix with hopefulness in their eyes. The elevator doors open on the 5th floor and there is a team waiting to greet us. The medic carefully dismounts the stretcher and allows the awaiting team to take over. One of the doctors looks at me and says, "Ma'am, we will do our best to save your husband." I nod in agreement and say to myself, "I pray he makes it through this so he can be my husband." The guard wheels me back to the emergency room to complete some paperwork. Sitting there, I remember just how much I hate hospitals; the smell, the stern and sometimes mean attitudes of the nurses, doctors, staff members and just the general atmosphere. Everyone is stone-faced, no one smiles, no one makes direct eye contact and getting answers is like pulling teeth. Sitting in this room makes me feel no different. The flowered green and pink wallpaper looks like it needed to be changed or upgraded 30 years ago. There is a T.V. mounted to the wall in the far right corner of the room with a display of a beach with blue waters, the sound of crashing waves coming through the very dull speakers. I stare at the screen for a brief moment wishing I was on a beach somewhere with Phoenix sitting next to me and the both of us are sipping some tropical drink with little umbrellas hanging off the side. I snap out of my thoughts when it hits me. I quickly open and start to fumble in my Celine bag in search of my cell phone. I realize that I have not contacted Auntie Hattie. Once I retrieve my iPhone and am ready to place my thumb on the button that identifies my thumbprint, the phone rings. I slide my index finger across the phone and place it up to my ear and answer, "Hello." The tears start to flow again as I hear Auntie Hattie's voice and I can't get a word out. "Baby I heard, I'm in the parking lot and will be inside in a few minutes," she says. Within seconds, she appears in front of me and bends down to embrace me. She whispers to me, "everything will be okay and we will pull through this. Phoenix is a fighter sweetheart. He will not let a bullet keep him from you or those babies," she says in a comforting voice. She loosens her embrace and I tell her that Phoenix was shot in the neck and his heart stopped in the ambulance on the way to the hospital. She smiles a half-weak smile and says, "He always was a show off baby, he'll be fine." Somehow when Auntie Hattie speaks those words, I believe she is trying to convince herself that in fact he will be fine. I start to wonder outside the deaths of his parents and twin sister, which is indescribable, what other tragedies Phoenix has suffered. He's been somewhat private, only giving me a little of his past. He always focuses on me and my issues and evades the questions regarding his past whenever I ask. I tell myself that Phoenix will pull through this and we will have our whole lives to discuss his past. Hattie asks if I was okay and if I needed a doctor to check me out. I know I should because that crazy ass Rocky kicked me in the stomach, but I told her I was fine. I felt pain at the time but I don't feel it anymore. My mind is telling me to get checked out but my heart is more focused on Phoenix. If Hattie knew I was kicked, she would force me to see a doctor.

Auntie Hattie excuses herself, breaking my thoughts. She walks over to the receptionist desk and asks the young woman sitting there if she can provide her with the whereabouts of her nephew. She also inquires about Ben. Oh my goodness, I am so focused on Phoenix that Ben slipped my mind. I feel really bad, how could I forget about Ben. When Auntie Hattie returns to where I am sitting, she gets behind the wheelchair I'm sitting in, starts to push me and says, "Come on baby, let's go check on the men we love." I look up and see a man with a white lab coat on standing in front of two white double doors at the end of the hallway. We head in the direction of the man. As we are on our way towards the man, I update Auntie Hattie on the other events that have happened. I tell her that 'X', Cameron and one of the undercover cops were killed and that Rocky shot CoCo and I don't know if she's dead or alive. As soon as those words leave my mouth, the waterworks start again. "How and why did this go so wrong?" I ask. She shakes her head and replies, "Sometimes things just happen and bad things happen to good people. It's just the way of this crazy world we live in. We can't explain why and we will drive ourselves crazy trying to figure out what we could have done differently for a better outcome. Let's not focus on what happened right now, we must be strong for Phoenix, Ben and CoCo. We will try to put this whole situation behind us," Why is she so calm? Why doesn't she seem worried? These are questions I ask myself. I'm trying to be optimistic but it's hard due to my past and how things generally turn out for me...tragically! I pray to God that this will be different. Auntie Hattie pushes my wheelchair as we follow the man in the lab coat to the elevator and he hits the 5th floor button. We ride in silence. The bell rings indicating that we reached our destination. Again, we follow the man as he leads us to a waiting room. He asks us to please wait here and someone will be with us shortly to give us an update. Auntie Hattie takes a seat next to my wheelchair. The waiting room is completely empty. There is a stale hospital smell that permeates through the air. There is an old coffee table with an array of magazines on it and a T.V. hanging in the corner at the back of the room. I lock the wheels on the wheelchair and stand, slowly wobbling over to the table and grab an outdated People Magazine. My mind is all over the place wondering what's going on with Phoenix, Ben and CoCo. I even think about Rocky and wonder what his status is. I really shouldn't give a shit but for whatever reason…I do. I want his ass to live so he can spend the rest of his life in prison. When I return to my chair, Auntie Hattie reaches over and grabs my hand. She looks at me and gives me a warm smile that kind of eases my mind a little, but not much. "Don't worry honey, God will work it all out. He has got us out of some serious situations before and there's no doubt that He will do it again. Remember, He won't put more on us than we can handle, and He will never leave us or forsake us," she says. I take in a deep breath then exhale, trying to let go of all the anticipation that has built up in my chest. "I pray you're right, Auntie Hattie," I reply. "I am, honey, I am." A few minutes pass and a young East Indian female doctor enters the waiting room and asks if we were Sydney Marshall and Hattie Davenport. We both nod with a yes. I try to stand and the doctor tells me to stay seated. Oh this can't be good, I think. She speaks, "Hello, I'm Dr. Kamdar and I'm the attending physician for Nicole (CoCo) Moore. Are you family members?" I began to speak when Auntie Hattie takes the lead. "Yes we are, I am her aunt and this is my daughter, her cousin Sydney. How's my niece Dr. Kamdar?" she asks. My heart was beating out of my chest waiting for the news. I thought it could not be good if she asked me to stay seated. "Doctor, please don't beat around the bush, please let us know if CoCo is alive or not," I blurted out. Auntie Hattie takes my hand and tells me to calm down and let the doctor speak. Dr. Kamdar begins to speak when we hear a "Code Blue" come over the hospital's speaker. She excused herself and quickly walks out of the waiting room. Auntie Hattie and I sat in silence for a few minutes when Detective Watson walks in. He enters and with hesitation leans over and hugs Auntie Hattie and me. He then sits down in a chair right across from us. He's silent. He then asks if we've heard anything. Again, Auntie Hattie takes the lead and fills him in on what just happened before the doctor left the waiting room after hearing the code blue call. The detective gets a call; he stands, excuses himself and exits the waiting room to answer the call. Just as he steps out, Dr. Kamdar steps back in the room. She pulls up the chair Detective Watson just sat in and faces both Auntie Hattie and I. "I'm sorry about that, I had to go check on that code blue patient. It's been a crazy day and it's never a dull moment here at county but another life was saved so I'm happy. Now back to your loved one. Ms. Moore suffered a gunshot to her abdomen, which she lost a great deal of blood. The bullet caused so much internal and female organ damage that we had to perform a complete hysterectomy and repair her small intestine. Because of the severity of her injuries we could not contact her next of kin and we had to make an emergency medical decision to remove her female organs. She appears to be rather young and we did not know her medical history so I hope she has a child or children because we had to do what we thought was right to save her life. Other than that, she will be under observation for the next few days but she should make a full recovery," she explains. Auntie Hattie and I exhale at the same time when Dr. Kamdar finished giving us the news. "CoCo, I'm sorry, Nicole, has a set of twins and has always expressed that she didn't want any more kids. She has the worst periods in the world, so trust me she will be happy," I reply. "That's a relief, I'm glad to hear that. There's nothing worse than to tell a young woman who does not have children that we had to give her an emergency hysterectomy and she will never be able to bear children," says Dr. Kamdar. "Trust me, she will kiss you when she wakes up. Speaking of, when can we see her?" I ask. Dr. Kamdar tells us she will be in recovery for a few hours then a nurse will come get us when she's ready for visitors. Auntie Hattie tells the doctor that we have a few more relatives in the hospital who were involved in the same incident and she would like an update on their status as well. The doctor looks perplexed and asks who the other patients are. "Phoenix Davenport and Benjamin Johnson," she states. Dr. Kamdar pulls a mini iPad out of her pocket and types something in the device. She looks up at us and asks our relationship to the patients. "Phoenix is my nephew, Sydney is his wife and Benjamin...Benjamin is my son."

Chapter 5

Stop the fucking press! I just heard a record scratch across an album, the world just stopped. Did she just say Benjamin is her son!? What the hell is going on? I ask myself. Dr. Kamdar then says, "You will need to speak to Dr. Coverton regarding your nephew's condition but your son needs a series of blood transfusions. He has a rare blood type, A-, and we're waiting for some blood donations from another blood bank because we are out here." "I'm A- as well, I will donate for my son," Auntie Hattie says, now with tears in her eyes. She looks at me with a single tear sliding down her face and says, "I'll be back honey, try to stay calm and I'll get an update ASAP." Auntie Hattie walks out with Dr. Kamdar and Detective Watson walks in. "What is all that about?" he asks. "Oh, you will not believe it if I tell you. This here is Sweeter than Honey". I fill in the detective on the bombshell Auntie Hattie just dropped and he has to sit down to process the news. I have to also process the news. How can Phoenix keep this kind of information from me? Does he know? While Auntie Hattie is donating blood for Ben I have the detective wheel me down the hall to the nurse's station to see if I can find this Dr. Coverton to give me an update on Phoenix's condition. The head nurse informs me that the doctor is in surgery with Phoenix and as soon as he can, he will come and update me on his condition. As we head back to the waiting room, I look up on a board that has a list of patients, their doctor's and room numbers. I spot two familiar names on the board, Rockland Foster and Nicole Moore. "That bastard Rocky is on this floor!" I say out loud. I turn to the detective and ask if he can get an update on Rocky's condition. He wheels me close to the wall and out of the way of everyone and their daily routines. I face the nurse's station so I can hear what is being said. "I'd like to get an update on Rockland Foster's condition please." "Are you a relative?" the nurse asks. "No, but I'm the detective on his case. There are two police officers outside of his room because once he is discharged, he's being released to the custody of the Oakland Police Department." The nurse turns around and reaches for a carousel of charts. She pulls the one that I assume belongs to Mr. Rockland Foster. She returns to the desk where Detective Watson stands and lays the chart on top of the counter. She flips through the pages and sort of giggles. "What's so funny?" Detective Watson asks. The nurse closes the chart and tells Detective Watson that Mr. Foster will be discharged later this evening. His injuries were not life-threatening; in fact, he only needs a few stitches but will need a great deal of dental work. Detective Watson looks confused as do I. "Can you please be more specific?" he asks. "In an attempt to kill himself, Mr. Foster must have placed the gun under his chin at an angle because when he pulled the trigger, the bullet went straight through his chin and out of his mouth shattering pretty much all of his teeth." says the nurse. The detective found that same giggle the nurse had. "I'm glad y'all find this shit funny," a voice says behind us. We all turn to see Keisha Foster, Rocky's ghetto ass sister standing with her arms folded across her 44DD's. "What the hell is so funny I said? And why is you giving dem my brother's info for? Where da hell is my brother at?" I thought...behind that preposition? Who the hell talks like that? I question myself. The nurse got serious and says, "Your brother is fine and in

47

protective custody." Detective Watson interjects and says, "You will not be able to see him until he is transferred to the Glenn Detention Facility and booked. Keisha walks over to me and tries to get in my face. The detective is at my side within a second. Keisha looks at him and sucks her teeth and tells me, "Bitch you are sponsible for dis shit, dis is all yo fault. Payback is a mother, bitch." I politely tell her I would recommend that she use dental floss to clear whatever is in her teeth and to take a class to learn correct English. I don't take kindly to threats, and I might have casts on my legs but you know where I live, so if want some shit to go down, I'm with it. Oh and don't let this LA face and Oakland booty fool you boo, I will stick my foot so far up your ass, my big toe will tickle your tonsils. Detective Watson tells Keisha that she needs to leave and she will be contacted when she can see her brother. With that, Detective Watson wheels me back to the waiting room. Auntie Hattie is standing there watching the whole incident. When Keisha stomps by her, Auntie Hattie says, "If you come anywhere near my family you're going to deal with more than a foot up your ass." She then pats the side of her purse and smiles at Keisha. She then turns around and walks in the direction of the waiting room. Auntie Hattie comes in the waiting room and sits next to me. She grabs my hand, takes her thumb and strokes it across the back of my hand. While doing this, she remains silent. My mind is racing a mile a minute trying to connect the dots. Just as Auntie Hattie starts to speak, a striking man walks in the waiting room wearing a surgical uniform. He stops and removes his surgical hat and stares at us. My mouth drops open. This man stands 6'3 and is a glass of dark chocolate milk. If I didn't know any better, he could pass for the British actor, Idris Elba. He walks over to me and says, "Hello Ms. Sydney Marshall." My mouth is still wide open. I finally find my words after a few seconds and reply, "Hello Brandon." Brandon turns and extends his hand to Auntie Hattie and says, "Hello. My name is Dr. Brandon Coverton." "Hattie Davenport," she replies.

Brandon and I have a history. I met him through a mutual friend when I was still living in Los Angeles. He was completing his first year of surgical residency at UCLA Medical Center. When we met, it was lust at first sight. I was young, younger than he by ten years, mature but young no less. I was fascinated with him because he was a doctor, handsome, and a pleasure to be around. He knew how to make me laugh and he knew how to take care of a women. He was romantic and spontaneous. Brandon allowed me to be me by encouraging and supporting me and never judging me. We connected on so many levels even though I was ten years his junior. We took many trips and he showered me with the finer things in life but most importantly...he respected me, or so I thought. We had a nice four-year romantic run and I really cared for this man. My age never was a problem for him as he treated me as if I were his equal. He told me he was in love with me but could not get too serious because of his career. I understood and was cool with the way things were with our situation or that's what I told myself to believe. The sex between us was amazing. He had what I call a 'tazor tongue.' This was a tongue that sent electric shock waves through my body when he flicked it across my clit. He loved for me to sit on his face and I called him the 'pussy monster,' you know

49

like the Cookie Monster likes to eat cookies, well Brandon loved to eat my cookies. Damn, I just had a flash back and my centerpiece is throbbing! "Stop it," I tell myself as the image of Phoenix appears in my head. I shake it off and try to continue on my stroll down memory lane with less dirty thoughts. I remember one trip we took up the coast to just get away and relax. Brandon had just finished a double shift and had a few days off. He was extremely tired so I suggested we postpone until he rested up. He, however, insisted we keep our plans. I drove and he slept. Once we checked into our hotel, The Fire Place Inn, in Carmel California, we both hopped in the shower then decided to take a nap before we went out for dinner. The Fire Place Inn was a villa that sat right at the Pacific Ocean. The sound of the crashing waves was so soothing and calming which hypnotized us into a deep slumber. We embraced each other as we slept, his arm around me and my head buried in his chest. I'm not sure how long we slept but as I was adjusting, I hear a soft whisper my ear. He calls me, "Baby, are you awake?" "Yes," I respond. "Then get your ass up here and sit on my face." He barks. I laugh and do as I'm told. It was just a short distance to his face but I was already anticipating his tazor tongue. Now this was some funny shit, as I sat on his face he quickly got me to where I needed to be. It didn't take long because he knew just how to suck, rotate, and flick his tongue. As I could feel the next orgasm coming, he suddenly stopped. I thought to myself, what the hell is he doing? Why did he stop? I'm almost there. I waited for a few seconds then began to move off his face. Just as I was moving, he started to suck again. Did this nut just fall asleep sucking me? I asked myself. As he

50

started again, he stopped again. I laugh to myself and try to remove myself again. Just as I did, he proceeds to suck again. I said, "Look here mister, you're clearly tired, so let's do this later after you get some more rest." My request fell on deaf ears because he proceeds again. The next time I pop off quickly so he couldn't catch me again. Again, I laugh to myself as he rolled over and went to sleep. It was the funniest thing, he was like a baby falling asleep feeding and when you tried to remove the bottle he'd latch on again. When we got up to get ready for dinner, I told him what he had done then told him I was not his pussy pacifier. We laughed about that for months. I think Brandon is reminiscing about the same thing right now because of the smile on his face and the glare he's giving me.

I stand and we exchange a friendly embrace. "My how we have grown," he says as he rubs my stomach in a rotating motion and lets out a slight chuckle. "Yes, I'd say so considering I have twins baking in there," I reply with an uncomfortable tone. Auntie Hattie clears her throat, stands and says with great authority, "I'm sorry to interrupt your little reunion, but do you have an update on my nephew?" Brandon looks embarrassed, releases me and turns to face her. "Yes. I apologize. Mr. Davenport lost a great deal of blood due to the gunshot injury to his neck. The bullet pierced his Internal Jugular (the Carotid Artery) enough to create some severe damage and is lodged in his Cervical Vertebrae. We were able to repair the jugular but he is still not out of the woods just yet. With the location of the bullet in the vertebrae, we are unable to remove it for fear of him being paralyzed. We will need to wait a few days until the swelling goes down to assess the situation at that point. We will run some additional tests to make sure his brain is functioning as it should but only time will tell the true magnitude of his injury."

Chapter 6

I sit back in the chair and bury my head in my hands and begin to sob uncontrollably. Dr. Coverton tells us that he is sorry he can't deliver better news; however, he is hopeful that Mr. Davenport will make a full recovery. Before he can catch himself, the words have exited from his mouth and he regrets what he has said because even in his best medical opinion he has no idea of the outcome and he just possibly gave these two women a false sense of hope. Dr. Coverton tells us that he will give us some time and check back with us in a couple of hours. He turns and walks out of the waiting room. Detective Watson comes over to comfort me, but Auntie Hattie tells him that she appreciates his support but she would like for us to be left alone for a while. Detective Watson understands and says as he's walking towards the door, "I will be available if you need me." He also informs us that he will be in the hospital until Rocky is released to his custody. I want to see Phoenix; hold him, kiss his lips, let him know that I am here and that I love him so much. I stand and start to wobble over to my wheelchair when Auntie Hattie grabs my hand and gently pulls me back to the chair. "Baby, sit," she says. "I need to see Phoenix," I cry. She comforts me and tells me I will as soon as he's out of recovery. "The nurse or the doctors will let us know when we can see Phoenix, CoCo and Ben," she whispers. I try and take the weight off by getting comfortable in the chair. I try to control my emotions but I am a wreck. I can't sit still. I keep thinking the worst but praying for the best. I feel like a little kid in church that has ants in her pants and has a bad case of the fidgets. Auntie Hattie places her hand on my knee to halt my movement. I turn and look at her and she smiles. She has an uneasy look on her face. She begins to speak and says, "While we're waiting honey, I might as well tell you about the situation with Ben, my son." She surely has my attention and I am still and quiet as a church mouse. I respond by saying she does not owe me an explanation, knowing deep down inside I wish I had a cup to catch all the TEA she is about to spill because for the life of me, this is one for the books and I would have never guessed such a thing. She began to speak again, "I was a junior in college in Texas. I was pretty popular around campus and being a member of a popular sorority, I had my fair share of fraternity and athletic parties. Well one particular night, I attended a frat party and had way too much to drink or so I thought. I found out later that I had been drugged with Rohypnol (the date rape drug). Anyway, I was raped by six guys that night and unfortunately got pregnant and had no idea which one of the assholes fathered the baby. It was the talk of the town because five of the guys were star football and basketball players. Some were expelled and other lost their scholarships, so needless to say, there were a lot of pissed off people. There was a video that circulated around campus, so proving the guys assaulted me without my consent was a no-brainer. It was a huge scandal at that time so my parents removed me from the school and it wasn't until a few months later that I found out I was pregnant. My family pretty much kept our little secret and no one knew but my parents and my brother, Phoenix's dad. My parents and I decided that it would be in the best interest for me and the baby, that I put him up for adoption. I was nineteen and would have turned twenty by the time the baby was born so I was old enough to care for the child but I was conflicted in raising a child created from such a horrific act. My brother loved me so much that he offered to raise the baby as his own so we could keep him in the family. I would not hear of it. He had his whole life in front of him and had just started to date Phoenix's mom. I could not allow that to happen. However, for years, I regretted not taking him up on his offer. But God always has a way of working things out.

I've known for some years that Ben was my son and it was pure fate that connected us together again. Ben has no idea that I'm his biological mother and I've wanted to tell him over the years but it was never the right time," Auntie Hattie explains with tears in her eyes as she relives this traumatic story. Wow, this is a great deal of information and I'm trying to process it all as well as hold my composure because it's such a sad story and my heart is going out to her. I can't even imagine the pain she has suffered. I mean, I can identify with being raped but I cannot comprehend having a baby and making the decision to part with the child you have just given birth to. She continues, "You're probably wondering how I know he's my son? I know because after fifteen hours of labor when he exited my body, I inspected every inch of his little chocolate body and the image was embedded in my memory immediately. During my inspection, I noticed that he had identical moles on his earlobes in the exact same place, it's like he had black stud earrings in his ears. I thought it was odd but I also thought it was cute at the same time. Of course that image has stuck with me as well as the way he smelled, his features, the way his little eyes opened

enough to look at me and the way he did, told me he would be okay and that he would understand I had to do what was best for him." Oh my God, I thought. I can no longer hold my tears and neither can Auntie Hattie. We sit there for what seems like hours not saying a word. She holds my hand and we cry. Finally, she reaches in her purse and hands me some tissue. I wipe my eyes, blow my nose and she does the same. I am at a loss for words. I don't know what to say. Auntie Hattie clears her throat and starts to speak again. "My father wanted all the guys tested for paternity to make the responsible one help raise the baby since he was dead against me putting the baby up for adoption. He agreed with my mother but in a private conversation expressed his true feelings and thought that I should keep the baby and he and my mother would be there to support me all the way. The decision tugged at my heart and knowing how my father felt made the decision even harder. I didn't know if I would hate the baby as he grew up. I didn't know if I would be hesitant to love. I thought it was best to put the incident, including the baby, behind me and move on with a fresh start. What did I know? I was twenty. I was wrong with all of my thoughts and feelings because from the moment I held him in my arms...I instantly fell in love! This is something I've obviously lived with for many years and the devastation has eaten away at me. I never married or had any more children; I'm not sure why, maybe it just wasn't in the cards for me. All of the guys were charged and sentenced for their crimes. So, imagine my surprise when Phoenix got into trouble some years back and Ben was his right hand man."
"Trouble? What kind of trouble was Phoenix in?" I

question. "That is a discussion you will need to have with Phoenix when he is better honey," she replies with pause. Okay, my mind is all over the place. What could he have done that she doesn't want to discuss with me. I guess she can see my mind racing so she grabs my attention back by calling my name and proceeds with her story. "The moment I saw Ben I knew he was my son because those identical moles on his earlobes were staring straight at me. The love for him that I tried so hard for years to suppress instantly reappeared. Ben and Phoenix have been very close friends for many years and there is a bond that will never be broken because of the things they have been through." Auntie Hattie is killing me with all the innuendos of things the guys have been through. I can't begin to imagine what the hell happened. I decide to put it out of my mind until I am able to have a conversation with Phoenix or Ben. Through heartfelt tears, she says that both her boys need to make it; they need to be strong as they have been in the past, she knows they will pull through this. She's really scaring me now. What the hell is going on or should I say, what the hell went on? I pray Phoenix doesn't have a crazy side that I don't know but will have to deal with the rest of my life since I am in love with him and carrying his seeds. Again, I try to put the thought out of my mind. I don't need any added stress right now. Auntie Hattie turns to me and says, "Ben needs to know I'm his mother, I just have no idea how I'm going to tell him. I almost lost him again and I cannot let another opportunity go by without telling him because life is too short and we are not promised tomorrow." Oh shit, there she goes again. What does she mean she almost lost him again? I ask myself. I reach over to hug her and try to console but again I'm not sure what to say. We are both in a bad place right now not knowing if the men we love are going to survive. We are both exhausted from the day's events and neither one of us can get comfortable in the waiting room chairs. We finally are in a semi slight slumber when Detective Watson gently wakes me up. "I'm sorry Sydney for waking you but I want you to know that Rocky is out of recovery and is stable enough for us to transport him to the Alameda County Jail for processing. I will call you once everything is done," he explains. Detective Watson turns to leave and I call out to him. He turns and looks at me with compassion in his eyes and waits for me to speak. "Just so you know… my brother is in county." He nods and walks out of the waiting room.

Chapter 7

A few minutes later, Detective Watson, four police officers and Keisha walk by the waiting room. The detective is in front, and there are two officers on each side of the gurney with Rocky. He is alert, looking around and his hands are cuffed to the side rails of the gurney's bed. Keisha is following behind. She rolls her eyes and gives me the middle finger as she walks by. She backs and says, "Watch your back bitch." She displays this evil smirk on her face that reminds me of Rocky when we were in the club and he had that same demented look on his face. I thought crazy runs in the family. I didn't have the energy to respond to her nonsense or threat, so I didn't. But Auntie Hattie tells her if she doesn't get her country, ghetto ass out of here, she will find herself in one of the hospital rooms recovering from being pumped full of lead. I laugh because she pats her purse and it reminds me of one of those Tyler Perry, Madea movies when the old lady pats her purse to let people know she has a gun in it. "Whatever you old bitch, ain't nobody scared of you," she shot back. "You need to be," Auntie Hattie replies and with that Keisha rolls her eyes again and walks away. I think to myself, Auntie Hattie is a gangster and I love this side of her. I am still laughing to myself when Dr. Kamdar interrupts my private entertainment. "Hello ladies," she sings. "I have some wonderful news. Nicole is awake and asking for you Ms. Marshall." I am so happy to hear this. I temporarily forget that I am in leg casts and need a wheelchair that I almost fall flat on my face. Auntie Hattie instructs me to sit in the wheelchair and she will wheel me to CoCo's room. We arrive to her room, the door is slightly ajar. I push the door

59

with my foot to open it wider. Once we're completely in the room, I see CoCo sitting up in the bed giving one of the nurse's pure hell. I think to myself, that girl is just fine. She looks in our direction and when she realizes it's us, she screams to the top of her lungs. I'm pushed close to her bed and I get out of the wheelchair and lean over in the bed to give her a hug as best I can with my leg situation and the tubes coming out of her arms. Auntie Hattie gives CoCo a kiss on her forehead and tells her she is glad she's doing well then excuses herself to get some coffee. "How are you sweetie," I ask. "Girrrlll, you know I'm good. I'm just happy to see you are okay. I can't believe that fat bastard shot me. If his ass ain't dead, I'm gonna kill em myself," she huffs. "I can't believe it either and no he is not dead. They just left the hospital taking him to county." "County!" CoCo shouts. "Oh hell, if he isn't dead he is now once Justin gets his hands on him. He's probably praying the whole way over there that they crash and he dies. Poor thing, I'm sure he's shitting bricks right about now, oh well serves him right. I hope they beat his ass!" she shouts again. "That's what I'm afraid of. You know I don't wish death on anyone and Rocky needs to pay for what he did but not at the hands of my brother. Justin only has two months left and I need him home. I don't want him in anymore trouble but I know once he finds out what happened, it's a wrap. CoCo goes on to say that Justin probably already knows because word travels fast from the outside in. I shake my head, trying to remove the thoughts from my mind for the time being. I want to focus on CoCo right now before I have to move on to the next issue. CoCo asks what happened to everyone else. I gave her a basic rundown that there were two undercover officers in the club and we had set up Cameron to come in so they could arrest him. But Rocky found out, shot both officers. One survived and the other didn't. There was more gunfire inside the club with some hoodlums Rocky hired to help him execute his plan. After the whole club shootout, Rocky took Ben, Cameron and Phoenix hostage and tried to get away. CoCo is so dramatic, she grabs her neck like she's clenching her pearls and gasps for air. I look at her, like really? "Girl, will you finish the damn story," she says. I tell her first off, this is not a story as we just lived this shit you crazy woman. I continue telling her what happened next with Rocky shooting everyone in the car including himself. "He shot Ben in the head, Phoenix in the neck and Cameron in the chest. Ben and Phoenix are out of surgery and we're praying they will be okay but Cameron didn't make it," I explain. "Damn," she says. "What the hell got into Rocky? Girl I would have never thought he would wig the hell out like he did. I guess love will make you do some crazy shit," she says. I tell her that Rocky's sister came to the hospital threatening me and that Ben is Auntie Hattie's son. "Wait, wait, wait. What the hell did you just say?" she screams. "Girl, are we living in a soap opera? 'As The Clubs Turns' or some shit like that. Again, I ask, what the hell is going on?" she says, hardly able to contain her laughter. I laugh a little at that part because it does seem like some T.V. drama or reality show. "I'll tell you more about that later because Ben doesn't know she's his mom." CoCo wants to know what Auntie Hattie is going to do and I respond with I have no idea. At that moment, Auntie Hattie re-enters the room with two cups of coffee and some snacks. I turn my attention back to CoCo and ask her how she is dealing with the fact that they had to give her an emergency hysterectomy. She was only 26; she does have twins and the periods from hell. She's expressed in the past that she doesn't want any more kids but when you're faced with something like this, one might feel differently. CoCo tells us she has her hands full with her two crumb snatchers and she has periods from hell so she doesn't need to have anymore of those either. She says she is sad that she isn't able to throw herself a (last period party). Auntie Hattie and I break out in laughter. Even though this woman has gone through this terrible ordeal, she still has a crazy sense of humor.

I ask about the twins and CoCo tells us that they are good and her grandmother is caring for them while she's in the hospital. She indicates that she just spoke to them right before we came in and they can't wait until she comes home. At that point, CoCo got serious and tears well in her eyes. "Sydney, I'm so glad I'm okay because if something would have happened to me, who would take care of my babies? You know granny does her best but they run circles around her," she says with a slight chuckle at the thought. "Promise me that if anything ever happens…you got me." I hesitate for a moment and reply, "I don't know CoCo. That will mean I'll have two sets of twins. Count them that is four kids. Bitch, are you crazy? Are you trying to kill me?" I try to say with a straight face. We all burst out laughing. I get serious and tell her nothing is going to happen to her but that's the last thing that she will ever have to worry about because I love her kids and they are already a part of our family. Then I ask her "ain't that what

Godparents are for anyway?" She laughs and says, "Oh yeah, you are their Godmother, I got that shit in writing." We sit and talk for a little while longer until CoCo starts to drift off to sleep. While we are getting ready to leave, she wakes and we tell her to get some rest and we will see her later. I kiss her on the cheek, Auntie Hattie does the same then we proceed to the door. CoCo tells me she loves me and I respond with, "I love you more." We are on our way back to the waiting room when Dr. Coverton is heading in our direction. Auntie Hattie stops wheeling my chair and waits for him to approach. When he does, he lets us know that Ben is awake and asking if Phoenix and Sydney are okay. He tells us that he told him he was not at liberty to discuss in detail the injuries but that you Sydney are okay and that he will let you know it was okay to see him. Dr. Coverton then explains that he will make a full recovery as the bullet was removed with no complications. He has some swelling due to the impact and the loss of blood but that will dissipate within a few days. They want to keep him for observation a few more days to make sure the swelling does in fact go down. We thank him for the update and then ask about Phoenix. He tells us that he is on his way to check his status now. He indicates he will locate us once he has the update. We head in the direction of Ben's room. Once we arrive, the door to the room is closed and there is a uniformed cop posted outside the room. You can see the curtain is drawn on the other side of the door. I ask the cop if we can go in and he says yes. He opens the door so we can enter. I want to peek around the curtain that provides privacy from the rest of the world. I call out to Ben to make sure he's decent before we come through, he doesn't answer. Auntie Hattie then peeks around the curtain to see Ben peacefully sleeping. We quietly come further in the room and she wheels my chair close to the right side of the bed. She then grabs a chair from the corner and puts it next to the other side of the bed. I gently hold his hand and want to lay my head down on the bed but before I do I look at him and one side of his face is pretty swollen. I remember Brandon saying it would be and he is expected to make a full recovery. I take comfort in knowing that Ben will be okay. I look over at Auntie Hattie and she's staring at Ben with tears in her eyes and sadness in her heart. My heart hurts for her. I'm sure she's thinking of the best way to tell him that she is his biological mother. "For you two to be the most beautiful women I know, you both look like you lost your puppies or something," Ben says in a weak raspy voice. We both are pulled from our thoughts and look at him. "Hey sleepy head, you had us worried," I say with a big smile on my face. "Oh don't worry about me. I'm a tough guy, this little ole gunshot can't stop me…I've been through worse," he replies. Okay, now here he goes with the innuendos. I can't wait to get to the bottom of whatever the hell they have been through. "Well, I'm not sure what you have been through but I sure am happy to see that you are okay right now." He smiles at me then asks about Phoenix. I update him on Rocky and Cameron then update him on Phoenix. "We are waiting for him to come out of recovery. The wait is killing us," I express. Ben has a relieved look on his face. "I want to see him," he says. "You will as soon as you get better," Auntie Hattie responds. "There's also some important things we need to talk about," she says with hesitation. She looks at me and I

64

tell her I can go find Dr. Coverton so she and Ben can have some privacy. Ben looks from side to side with a perplexed look on his face. "I thought you said Phoenix was okay," he says with a look of worry. Wow, Auntie Hattie didn't waste any time with wanting to tell him. I guess she's saying it's no better time than the present. I better make my fast get away before she loses her nerve. Ben and Phoenix have been friends for more than 10 years and have been thick as thieves ever since. Auntie Hattie has known that Ben was her son the second she laid eyes on him when Phoenix brought him home from college one holiday, I think she said Thanksgiving. When Auntie Hattie saw the birthmarks, she was speechless. She immediately told her brother, Phoenix's dad, to take a good look at Ben. When he did, he also remembered the mole birthmarks on the earlobes. At that moment, he knew that his nephew was standing right there in front of him, in the flesh, in his house, and he was overcome with emotion.

Chapter 8

Auntie Hattie, her brother and parents were the only ones who knew of this situation with Ben. She thinks that the reason Ben and Phoenix are so close is because they are cousins and the same blood runs through their veins. "Uh hello, does somebody wanna tell me what the hell is going on?" Ben says. Auntie Hattie clears her throat and says, "Ben, I have something very important to tell you. Now I don't want you to get upset. I want you to listen until I'm done. Do you understand?" Ben tries to sit up in the bed but realizes he doesn't have as much strength as he thought. I find the button on the side of the bed that raises the back of the bed. As the bed is rising, he looks at me and smiles as to say thank you. Ben turns to Auntie Hattie and tells her to continue. She continues by telling him that she has wanted to have this conversation but didn't know when the right time was and that she was afraid of the outcome. However, in light of recent events, she realizes that life is too short and doesn't want to wait any longer. She starts her story and tells him just as she told me earlier but with more tears and much more regret. Ben lay there taking it all in with tears in his eyes. He never interrupts her, just listens very attentively. Auntie Hattie ends the story with, "Giving you up was the hardest thing I ever had to do and if I had it to do over again you would have been in my life from day one. I pray you understand that under the circumstances I did what I thought was best to do. My heart has been heavy for the past 28 years and I've wished you a happy birthday every January 25th. I can never make up for the past and I know you love your parents, which is one reason I didn't want to tell you, I didn't want to ruin your life." "Why now?" he interjects. "I almost lost you for the second time. The doctor said you needed blood. I knew your blood type and I felt it was my opportunity to help save your life. I did what any mother would have done given the chance." Ben wipes his eyes, clears his throat and says, "Well it's about time…Mom." Hattie and I are both shocked and speechless at the same time. "Excuse me?" she says. "It's about time…mom," he says once again. "How did you know?" she responds. Ben begins to explain that when he was a young boy his adoptive parents told him where he came from and even though it was a closed adoption they knew who his biological mother was. There was a stipulation in the adoption agreement that when he turned 18 years of age, he had the right to initiate contact with her if she felt the same way and wanted to connect. They felt that it was important for him to know and he had the option to do something with the information or not. Ben's parents raised him from birth, and they were his parents but his mom felt the need for him to have the information and felt like they didn't want to hide the truth from him. They love him and he loves them and that will not change but Ben had the information to do what he saw fit. Ben tells us that he didn't want to know who she was but when he turned 18 and was off to England for the student exchange program, he asked his mom what his biological mother's name was and if she had a picture of her. She told him his mother's name is Henrietta Davenport but people call her (Hattie). He also asked about his biological father and was told that his mother was raped in college by 6 guys and didn't know who the father was and this is the reason she gave him up for adoption. Ben drops another bomb on us. He tells us that his adoptive father is an older brother to one of the guys who raped Auntie Hattie. He indicates that his adoptive father did not find out that the baby was a product of the rape that his little brother was involved in until years later. Once he found out, he told my adoptive mother and they immediately had me DNA/Paternity tested. My adoptive father told me the wait for the results was the hardest thing he ever had to wait for but it didn't matter what the results were, although it would be nice if his blood ran through my veins. The results finally came back and it was declared that I was not related to my adoptive father. He treated me no different; in fact I think he loves me more.

When Ben finished telling us this story, Auntie Hattie was crying uncontrollably. Ben also explains that he had no intentions on looking for her and that he was very happy and loves his parents dearly. He also includes that he understands why she did what she did and was not mad at her at all, instead he loves her for looking out for his safety. It wasn't until he went to college in England and met Phoenix, who was his roommate that Ben made the connection. They were exchanging stories about their families and Phoenix mentioned his Auntie Hattie. He tells us he knew Phoenix's last name and thought it was a coincidence that his aunt and his biological mother have the same name. He put two and two together and realized that Phoenix's aunt and his biological mother are one in the same. Ben then tells Phoenix the story of his life and Phoenix pulls out pictures of his aunt and he and Ben compare the photos they have and came to the conclusion that they are the same woman. They both thought this is some crazy shit and decided they would keep this newfound information to themselves and they have been extremely happy to know that they are first cousins. "When Phoenix brought me home for Thanksgiving, it was confirmed when we saw the way you reacted. Phoenix kept his promise and didn't say anything. We agreed it was best to wait and see if and when you would ever approach me. Phoenix will be happy to know the cat is out of the bag and we can be free from the secret we've known for 10 years," he laughs. Auntie Hattie is still crying and Ben holds out his arms to embrace her. She walks over to his bed and leans over so he could wrap his arms around his mother and she did the same, wraps her arms around her son. They've hugged before but for some reason this hug is very different. Wow, this is way too much drama for me. So far I have seen two people I love but I have not been able to see my true love. I need to see Phoenix. I need to make sure he is okay. I've never been so scared in my life, not because of the drama that unfolded at the club but because I can very well lose the one man I truly love. I tell Ben and Auntie Hattie that I'm going to find Dr. Coverton to see if I can get an update on Phoenix. I wheel myself to the nurses' station, "I can't wait until these damn casts are off my legs," I think to myself. I reach the nurses' station and inquire about Dr. Coverton's whereabouts. This five-foot nothing little Filipino male nurse lets me know he's doing rounds and he will let him know I'm looking for him. He suggested I wait in the waiting room down the hall and he'll inform the doctor that I'm there waiting. I turn my wheelchair around and head in the direction of the waiting room…yet again. I'm so tired of waiting, and I'm getting hungry and sleepy, I think to myself. A few minutes later Dr. Coverton walks in the waiting room flashing that million-dollar smile, the one that makes my 'centerpiece' moist; even after so many years, he seems to still have that effect on me. I try to dismiss the feeling I am having at the moment of sitting on his face and letting him do what he wants to do. But I quickly dismiss the thought because one of the twins kicks the shit out of me that almost makes me lose my breath, bringing me back to my senses. Dr. Coverton pulls up a chair and sits next to me. He pulls the chair a little closer and asks, "Sydney, why are you calling me Dr. Coverton? You know we are beyond the formalities, so please do me a favor and call me Brandon. It's weird hearing you call me Dr. Coverton." I smile and tell him I am trying to be professional. "Woman please," he says with a slight giggle. He hands me a brown paper bag. "What's this?" I ask. "Open it." I open the bag and he must have been reading my mind because it is just what the doctor ordered. He has an egg sandwich, BBQ chips and a bottle of water. "Thank you so much. How did you know I needed this?" I ask as I rip the sandwich package open and take a bite, feeling like this has been the only thing I've eaten in days. "I didn't. I was taking a shot in the dark because of your situation; you need your energy and need to eat." "I do and thank you so much," I reply as I finish the half of my sandwich. Brandon stares at me for a moment, looking me up and down. He then asks, "What happened to your legs?" I give him the breakdown of the chain of events that brought us here today. He is shocked and cannot believe the stalking, choking, and being ran over with a car can happen to one person in a short period of time. He also could not believe I am having a baby. I corrected him, "Babies, I'm having twins remember?" "Wow! Twins, yes how can I forget? I'm still in shock," he says. Brandon then asks about Phoenix. He wants to know how long we've known each other, does he come from a good family, can he provide for me, and more importantly, do I love him. I tell him to slow down with all the questions and that he should have been a detective instead of a doctor. He laughs. "To answer your questions Mr. Nosy pants, Phoenix and I have known each other just shy of a year. Yeah, I know that's not a long time but things are different with him. I've never felt this way about someone before and you know how guarded my heart is." Brandon nods his head up and down indicating he understands what I'm expressing to him. I continue to answer his questions. "He's smart, caring, understanding, loving, attentive, and successful. He comes from a good family and takes great care of me; mentally, physically, and financially. Although, you do know I can take care of myself?" I express. "Yes I do. I'm glad you have found someone you can share your life with. You deserve to be happy and to have someone who loves you unconditionally and shares your same interest. Even though you and I had a great time together and you know I cared for you, I knew I couldn't give you all of me. I couldn't give you what you truly needed and deserved but you can best believe that if this situation was different and you were not in love with someone else and having their babies, you can bet your pretty little ass that your ass would be mine. I'm happy if you're happy." We both laugh. He then says, "Now that we have reconnected, there's no reason why we can't be friends and keep in contact." I tell him one step at a time and remind him he is my boyfriend's doctor and I'm not sure how he would react to me reconnecting with an old flame.

"You're probably right. We'll work on getting Mr. Davenport well and work on our friendship later," he replies. "Speaking of Mr. Davenport, is it possible for me to see him now?" I ask. Brandon reaches in his lab coat pocket and pulls out his mini iPad. He types some information in and a few seconds later his cell phone rings. He answers it. He says, "I see," in acknowledgment to what is being said on the other line. He disconnects the call, looks at me and smiles. "Let's go see your Mr. Davenport." Brandon stands and positions himself behind me and begins pushing my wheelchair. We reach a room that reads (Recovery Room 6) on the outside of the door. Brandon moves from behind me to push open the door that is slightly ajar, he then gets behind me to proceed through the door.

Chapter 9

My heart drops yet again. Phoenix lies there with tubes coming out of everywhere. There is a nurse standing over him monitoring the machines that house the tubes and writes something on her pad. She either did not hear us come in or she is very focused on what she is doing. Brandon locks the wheels on the wheelchair walks over to the nurse and whispers something in her ear. The nurse looks back at me and smiles. She finishes up what she's doing then steps away from Phoenix so Brandon can evaluate his condition. In the brief moment there's a clear view of Phoenix, he looks over at me sitting in my wheelchair. He doesn't speak because he has a tube coming from his mouth that connects to another from his neck. He has tears in his eyes, and so do I. I am already distraught but seeing him like this makes it worse. He weakly lifts his hand to beckon me to come closer. Brandon tells him to give him a second as he wants to check his vitals, tubes, and whatever else he needs to do. After he's done assessing Phoenix, he pushes me close to Phoenix's bed. Brandon then lets us know he will leave us to have some privacy but will be a page away if we need him. I thank him and he leaves the room. Once he's out of the room, I grab hold of the side of the bed, using the rail for support to stand. I first adjust the bedrail so I can get closer to my man. I let the rail down then lean over to give him a kiss on the side of his mouth, then his cheek, then his forehead. Phoenix has his eyes closed as he has been waiting for these kisses for a long time. Tears flow down his cheeks and I wipe them away. He takes his hand and rubs the side of my face. I take his hand and kiss the palm and the back of his hand.

Phoenix takes his hand from mine then moves it close to my stomach. I move in a little closer so he can touch my stomach. He rubs it in a circular motion and he looks like he has a frown on his face. I place my hand on his and tell him the babies are fine. I think he tries to exhale and his face relaxes a bit. He pats the bed for me to lie next to him. I comply after I lower the bed for me to get in. The bed is big enough for me to lie next to him comfortably. Even though he smells like everything hospital; meds and dried blood, I'm still glad to be lying next to him right now. After a few minutes of lying still next to the man I love, my cell phone rings. I retrieve it from my pocket and see that it's Auntie Hattie. "Hi, Auntie Hattie. I'm with Phoenix and he's awake. He's in recovery room 6 and I'm sure he cannot wait to see you." I power off my phone and put it back in my pocket. A few seconds later, here enters Hattie. She walks to the other side of the hospital bed and gives Phoenix a kiss on his forehead. He squeezes her hand, letting her know he is okay. We are both silent for a few minutes until our silence is broken by Brandon when he walks in the room. He walks on the side of the bed where Auntie Hattie is and politely asks if she could move to the side so he can check Phoenix. She does as he asks and waits patiently for him to report and move so she can get close to her nephew again. Brandon tells Phoenix that he is going to remove the tube from his mouth but the tube in his neck will remain for a little while longer. Phoenix nods his head slightly, acknowledging what Brandon has just said to him. Brandon proceeds to remove the tape from around his mouth, which is holding the tube secure in its place. I turn my head because the sight of all of this is making me queasy. Brandon tells Phoenix he's getting ready to start and as he pulls the tube out, Phoenix starts to cough and gag until the tube is all the way out. Brandon hits the call button to summon the nurse. Her voice comes through a speaker that's connected to the bed. "Yes, this is Nurse Elaine, how can I help you?" "Elaine, its Dr. Coverton, bring Mr. Davenport some crushed ice please." Within moments, the nurse walks in with a few paper cups and a pitcher of crushed ice. Brandon is ready to give him the ice when Auntie Hattie interrupts and offers to give Phoenix the ice just as I am about to stand and give aid to my man. Brandon gives the cup of ice after he pours some into the cup. Auntie Hattie looks over to me and says, "Baby, I got this. I need you to rest." I position myself back in the chair and let her carry on. Phoenix turns to me and I wink at him. After a few cups of ice, Phoenix tries to talk and Brandon tells him to try not to talk and that his throat will be a little sore for a few days. He also says to suck the ice and let it melt in his mouth. Phoenix opens his mouth and she puts a spoonful in and he closes his eyes and moans like the ice is chocolate or sex. He opens his mouth again waiting for more and Auntie Hattie and I laugh because he looks like a baby being fed and the food is not coming fast enough. Auntie Hattie repeats this until the first cup is finished. She asks him if he wants more and he shakes his head no. He clears his throat and tries to speak. Auntie Hattie puts her finger up to his lips and tells him not to speak, to get some rest and there will be plenty of time for him to talk. Auntie Hattie leans in close and kisses him on the forehead again. She pulls the chair close to the bed, sits, pulls a book out of her bag and proceeds to read. Phoenix smiles at his aunt then looks at me and smiles. He looks like he's fighting to stay awake. "Babe, please get some rest, I'll be right here by your side until it's time for you to leave this place. He shakes his head, closes his eyes and off to sleep he went. I get in my wheelchair and wheel myself out to the nurses' station. I ask one of the nurses behind the desk if she could page Dr. Coverton. Five minutes later Dr. Coverton meets me in the hallway. I ask him if he can give me an update on Phoenix's condition and when he will be able to go home. Brandon says, "Phoenix is recovering well. He is strong, strong-willed and I believe he can be released within two days considering he stays on the road to recovery. We also want to make sure he does not get any infections. "How will you be able to care for him in your condition?" he says. "In my condition?" I reply. "I'm pregnant and my legs are broke, believe me I will get it done. Plus my casts will come off in 3 days and I'll have Auntie Hattie to help me as well. I've had these things on for 16 weeks; it's time for them to come off." I reply. We both laugh. I thank Brandon for the update. He hugs me and I proceed to wheel myself back into the room with Phoenix. "It's really good to see you Sweet and Low". I stop the wheelchair and turn to look at him. He has this wicked smile on his face that gives me goose bumps on my arms. "What did you say?" "I said, it is really good to see you..." I stop him just before he says it again. "I heard you the first time!" I snap! How inappropriate I think, but it did take me back to when we were dating. Brandon used to call me 'sweet & low', his reason was when he craved something sweet he could get it from me but he had to get down 'low' to get it. Use your imagination people. So needless to say, I had a flash back and got chills and moist at the same time when he called me that. "Hello," he says. I snap out of the past and give him my middle finger then continue to wheel myself back to the direction of Phoenix's room. I'm sure Brandon got a kick out of that because he is just an arrogant asshole. I make my way back to my man's room and the curtain is drawn and the door slightly ajar. I stop right at the curtain. I hear Auntie Hattie talking. I'm not sure if she's on the phone or talking to Phoenix. I wait for a few moments before I enter but pause when I hear Auntie Hattie say, "You have to tell her. You cannot build a relationship with someone and they don't know the truth about who you really are. You have to be completely honest with her baby. You know she loves you and will understand your past just as you understand and accepted who she is. Neither one of you are perfect, no one is but trust me you cannot keep this part of you inside, you will need to have a conversation with her so you can move on." She continues, "I've been keeping a secret for years and it damn near killed me. I cannot keep this a secret any longer. Life is too short baby and you have finally found a woman that you truly love. I have never seen you like this with any woman, she compliments you and you two are meant to be together. Ben knew what he was doing when he took you to that strip club, he knows you and what's best for you," she expresses. "If you like, I can be with you when you speak with Sydney. She will understand and not judge you. We all have a past, shit, and a present for that matter. I know where she came from. I know about her parents and her childhood and I know what she does or did for a living. So, I doubt if she of all people will judge you. She is a real

77

sweetheart honey and I commend her for the person she is. I love the fact that she is real. I love the fact that she has her own. I do agree with her sister and believe she is way too smart to be dancing at a club but again I appreciate her hustle and how she really doesn't need you nor does she give a shit about your millions. The moment I had the first conversation with her...I knew she was the one. Don't get me wrong sweetheart, I have fallen in love with her and she's carrying our bloodline, so regardless of her profession or your imperfections, you two are good for each other. I see the way you two look at each other. I've never seen you this caring and loving with any woman besides your sister, me and your mom, but obviously you know what I'm talking about so open up to her and let her know who you are. Furthermore, she has opened up to you and told you her fears and explained her demons. It's fine time that you do the same," she explains.

Chapter 10

What the hell is going on, I think. Tell me what, I ask myself. What has he done? What does he have to hide? These are all the questions that are floating in my head. I know I've asked certain questions and he's either ignored me or changed the subject. Just as I'm asking myself more questions, I get a sharp pain in my stomach that brings me out of my thoughts. It's now or never, as I decide it's a good time for me to enter the room completely. They both turn to me and are probably thinking how much did I hear and how long I've been there. I break the ice by saying, "Well hello you two. What's going on because you both look like you swallowed a canary? I'm glad to see you are awake babe," I say in my best chipper voice. I wheel myself over to his bed, stand and kiss him on the cheek. He taps his lips for me to kiss him there. I lean back over and comply with my man's wishes. To my surprise, when my lips touch his, he gives me one of the most passionate kisses I've ever had from him. Now, I've gotten some wonderful kisses from him but this one was different. This kiss sends chills through my body. When our kiss comes to an end, he says, "Hi baby," in a weak, raspy voice. "Hi yourself. Are you comfortable? Do you need anything to eat? How do you feel?" I ask before he could even answer the first questions. Phoenix smiles and says, "I'm fine babe. I'm more concerned about you and our babies." "The babies are fine," I reply as I feel another sharp pain tear through my body once again. I do a really good job at hiding the pain because I don't want to worry him plus I don't know what's going on myself. I look over at Auntie Hattie and she somehow seems to see right through me and says, "Sydney, it's been a long day and we all have been through so much, why don't we let Phoenix get some rest and let me take you home to get some rest as well. Ben and CoCo are doing good so I think we can leave them to rest as well and can come back in a couple of hours to check on them. I'm sure you would like to get off your feet and have a shower and some fresh clothes." What I would like to do is, stay right here next to my man, I thought. "No, I'm fine. I will ask the nurse to bring me an extra bed or a recliner chair and I'll rest up here," I respond. Phoenix turns to me and pleads that he's fine and that he's not going anywhere for the next few days so he really wants me to go home and get some rest. He tells me he needs me healthy and strong and does not want me stressing, so as not to cause harm to the babies or me. "Okay, if you insist. I guess I'll go home so you can rest," I reply, with hesitation in my voice. "By the way, your casts are coming off soon right?" He asks. "Yes, in 3 days and I can't wait." Another sharp pain shoots through my body, this time slightly taking my breath away. This time Phoenix notices my distress. "Baby, are you okay?" "Yes. I guess I'm more tired than I thought." Auntie Hattie kisses Phoenix on the forehead and tells him we will see him later and that she is going to stop to check on Ben on our way out. Before we leave the room Phoenix asks about the status of the others involved in the incident. I give him the abbreviated version and tell him that CoCo is recovering from her injury. She had an emergency surgery resulting in a complete hysterectomy, but she will be fine and is happy about the hysterectomy believe it or not. Ben is also recovering from his injury and he will be fine as well. Rocky is recovering in jail and unfortunately

80

Cameron didn't make it. There are a few more causalities including one of the officers. Phoenix closes his eyes as if saying a silent prayer. "This went so wrong. No one was to get hurt. I thought this was a solid plan to capture Cameron. No one would have ever thought that Rocky would do such a thing. God please forgive us for our mistakes and for the senseless lives lost. To make things worse, Cameron is not even here for me to apologize to," he says. "I need to talk to my best friend," he says. "Get some rest babe and in a few hours you can call his room, he's in room 320," I respond. Auntie Hattie tells him once everyone is home and well, we can discuss this at that time. "There are a lot of things we need to discuss," she says to Phoenix with a stern look. He acknowledges her comment with a head nod.

My mind is racing a mile a minute wondering what in the world they're talking about. I guess I'll just have to wait and see. We check in on Ben and CoCo on our way out and they both are resting peacefully. Once we reach the front door of the hospital to exit, we are hit with every news station in the Bay Area. Detective Watson is about to give a statement when a reporter notices me and yells, "There's Sydney Marshall, Cameron Wilkerson's girlfriend!" Now all eyes are on me. All reporters leave from their position in front of the podium where the detective stands and head in my direction blurting out question after question. "Ms. Marshall, how are you? Did Cameron break both your legs? Did he shoot your friends and club goers? How many people died at the hands of Cameron Wilkerson? Was he trying to kill you? Did he snap and that caused him to go to Delaney's and was this result of this violent outburst? We hear that you are pregnant with his twins and will you be able to care for them now that he is dead?" All these questions are sending my head into a tailspin. There are a few more questions that are being screamed at me but these are the ones that stick out. This is so overwhelming and if I could get up and run, I would. But I can't and Auntie Hattie yells, "She has no comment, now get the hell out of our way or I will personally run over each and every one of you with this wheelchair!" Detective Watson comes to our rescue and tells the reporters that he will be answering all questions. The reporters hesitate but make a pathway so we can get through. Auntie Hattie nudges forward, forcing them to move. We finally make our way through the crazy crowd and to the car. Once Auntie Hattie helps me in the car and gets in herself, I lose it. I place my hands over my face to somehow slow down, cover up, or stop the tears. It wasn't helping. The tears just keep coming and I am crying so hard that it's hard for me to breathe. Auntie Hattie leans over and says, "That's it sweetheart, let it all out. It's good to cry. You have been trying to be so strong and I could see your breaking point coming. Don't hold anything back and once it's all out, you'll feel much better. It's okay to be strong but it's also okay to be vulnerable at the same time. I know you think you can carry the world on your shoulders and handle any and everything, but sweetheart sometimes things are just out of your control. When things are out of your control you have to learn how to deal with certain situations. God will not put more on you than you can handle. He loves you and Phoenix, you two and the rest of the folks will get through this," she expresses.

"Really!?" I scream through my downpour of tears. "Well, I think you got it wrong. Because if God really didn't want to give me more than I can handle, why have I had to handle a great deal of shit? It was too much to handle my father's friend raping me at the age of nine. It was too much to handle when my baby brother shot and killed the same man. It was too much to handle when my parents didn't protect my siblings or me. It was too much to handle when my parents were killed due to their lifestyle and the retaliation of my brother killing one of their own. It was too much to handle when my sister had to give up her life to raise my brother and I. It is too much to handle to live my life not trusting anyone and believing that everyone is out to get you. Now it's too much to handle that I have finally found what I believe to be the man of my dreams and he's lying in a hospital bed with a gunshot hole in his neck and is near death because of me. And you can best believe it will be too much for me to handle being responsible for these lives I have growing inside of me. So with all due respect, I must have been absent the day God told everyone else that He would not give them more than they can handle or bear because clearly I didn't get that memo. The things I have gone through and am going through, no one person should have to deal with. I have been trying to handle all of my sad life's stories for years but again it's too much to handle! The tragedy that always strikes the ones I love," I passionately express. Auntie Hattie sits there and stares at me for a moment before she speaks. "Sydney, I can't imagine what you've been through but the operative word is 'through' and there is nothing to be ashamed of because none of it was your fault. You were a child and all of what you went through was out of your control. Bad things happen to good people. Unfortunately life experiences shape us into who we are today. We have the choice to continue to live in the past and hold on to all of our shit, or to make the decision to get help, forgive, forget and move on with our lives. Holding on to the past prevents us from progress, it prevents forgiveness and it prevents us to love whole-heartedly. In order for you to love Phoenix and love the twins, you need to work on forgiveness. Now sweetheart here's the difficult part, you are going to have to dig deep into your soul to do this because you cannot ask for forgiveness from dead people, so you will have to forgive them in light of the situation. If you don't, then you will be stuck in that mental state forever. As I said, bad things happen to good people and you have to realize and believe that none of this is your fault. You were a child and had no control over the stupid actions of insane adults. Sydney, they say shame controls every aspect of human behavior. It's about who we believe we are. But in the end, we can't hide the truth, it's right there for the world to see. Our shame can choke us, kill us and rot us from the inside, if we decide to let it. Don't let that happen to you baby," she says, now with just as much of a tear downpour as I have. I believe she is not only talking to me...but talking to herself as well.

Chapter 11

Auntie Hattie delivered a serious blow. She spoke volumes to my life and basically said everything I have been thinking about and feeling for years. I've been dealing with all of my life's misfortunes and I realize that I need help. The problem is that I've been thinking I can fix the shit myself; when all I do is make matters worse. I make a mental note to find a good therapist to call. Amber, I'm sure she can recommend someone. Oh shit, I need to call Amber! I'm sure she's worried out of her mind. Then I remember she and her husband are out of the country for a well-deserved vacation. I'm glad she's not here now that I think about it because she would be driving me crazy. Auntie Hattie dries her eyes, puts the key in the ignition and backs out of the parking stall. I am mentally and physically drained. I just want a hot shower and a nap. Some food will be good as my stomach is growling. I'm sure it is going to be hard for me to relax with Phoenix and everything else on my mind. Another sharp pain shoots through my body, which pulls me away from my thoughts. These pains have been happening all day. It's probably stress and I'm sure they will go away once I get some rest. Auntie Hattie and I ride in silence all the way to the Fairmount. Phoenix's apartment at the Fairmount Hotel is like my second home. He and I have had multiple conversations about me moving in. I'm hesitant to give up my place. I mean, what if things don't work out between us and I have nowhere to go. I doubt that will happen as far as not having anywhere to go because I'll always have a stash of money and a plan B, that's just the way I roll. What I should do is go ahead and move in with Phoenix because I will need the help from him and Auntie Hattie when the babies get here. I can have CoCo and her kids move into my place; it's in a better neighborhood and she can save money because I won't charge her anything for living there. Yes, that's what I'll do. It's a great idea and I'll let her know the next time I speak with her. We finally make it back to the hotel. The valet opens my door to help me out. I tell Auntie Hattie I'm fine with crutches and will not need the wheelchair. I place the crutches under my arms and head to the entrance of the hotel. A few people behind the registration desk send smiles and waves. I smile back and keep on my journey to the elevator. Auntie Hattie is right behind me and reaches me just as the elevator opens. We both pull out our penthouse key cards to insert it in the slot that allows us access to the 18th floor. Auntie Hattie beats me to the slot. After we exit the elevator and enter the apartment, I tell Auntie Hattie that I'm going to take a shower. She tells me to take my time and that she will cook us something to eat. I wobble down the hallway to the master bedroom. I drop the crutches and begin to remove my clothes. I am naked as the day I was born and make my way to the bathroom. I turn the shower on to allow the water to get hot. I sit on the toilet to relieve my bladder that the twins just love to rest on and watch as the steam begins to rise. There is a remote on the sink next to the toilet. I pick it up, hit the power button and immediately soft jazz starts to permeate through the air. I finish on the toilet, wipe, flush and pull the casts shower protectors on my legs that Phoenix has made for me. I reflect on the current events and a since of panic rises in my soul. I tell myself to relax and that everything is going to be okay. I step in the shower and let the hot water hit my face. The water is as hot as I can take it and it feels so good. The beads of water are thrusting against my body and the twins start to do what feels like summersaults and my stomach is moving like an alien is trying to exit. I step back from the water and take a seat on the seat that's in the shower. I stand and move under the water again and the twins start again. I guess it's safe to say they don't like the water beating on my stomach. I finish showering regardless to the battle that's going on inside me. I turn the water off, step out the shower, dry off and wrap a large Kate Spade bath towel around my body. I grab some Bath and Body Works Japanese Blossom lotion out of the cabinet and head to the bedroom. I sit on the edge of the bed and remove the casts shower protectors and lotion the top part of my thighs and my feet. I think about how happy I will be when these damn casts come off. I hear a slight knock on the door. "Just a second," I yell out. I guess Auntie Hattie didn't hear me because she came strolling in. She sits on the chaise in the sitting area of the master bedroom and is apparently comfortable with me sitting on the bed butt naked. I reach for the towel under me to cover my body. Seeing that I was in fact uncomfortable, she apologizes for coming in and lets me know that the food was ready and leaves the room. I slip on some sweats and one of Phoenix's t-shirts and some socks. I pull my hair up into a high bun and make my way to the kitchen. As soon as I step out of the bedroom, the aroma hits me. I can't tell exactly what it is but it smells divine. There is soft classical music playing in the background and Auntie Hattie is humming to the beat. She sees me entering the kitchen and instructs me to have a seat. I do as I'm told.

She fusses about for a few more seconds then turns to me and says, "I hope you're hungry sweetheart. I just whipped something up quick so you can eat and feed my babies." Are you kidding me, I think? Her something quick was turkey meatloaf, mashed potatoes, and cabbage. We say grace, and dive in. I feel like I have not eaten in years. I clean my plate in no time and Auntie Hattie laughs and says, "I guess you were hungry." She tells me she will take care of the dishes and she wants me to go get some rest. I waddle to the living room, grab the remote and hit the power button. I let my head rest on the couch as a pain shoots through my body. The pain was the worst of the pains I had felt yet and I am not able to contain my composure. I let out a loud, excruciating scream. I guess it startled Auntie Hattie because she drops a plate that shatters on the floor. She yells, "Sydney!" and comes running to the living room. Tears are running down my face and I'm holding my stomach. You can see the fear in her face. "What's wrong honey? Is it the babies?" she questions. I cannot answer her for I am in far too much pain. She runs in the kitchen and picks up the wall unit phone and calls 911. She's running around the apartment looking for her purse, all the while asking me where my purse is. She's screaming, "Hold on sweetheart everything is going to be okay! The ambulance is on the way and I'm calling your doctor". Minutes later, she opens the door to the Fairmount Hotel manager, the fire department and paramedics. They're asking me questions, which again I cannot answer because I'm in so much pain. I feel something wet between my legs and think I peed my pants because of the pain. I hear the paramedic ask how far I was in my pregnancy. Auntie Hattie answers 29 weeks with twins. One paramedic is on his walkie informing and updating the hospital as to what is going on. The other paramedic says, "Let's get her to the hospital, she's hemorrhaging." Two firefighters assist the paramedic and gently place me on the stretcher. Auntie Hattie is praying and holds my hand as they wheel me out of the apartment and into the elevator. She tells the manager to lock up the apartment for her and he acknowledges her with a nod. I am scared shitless. I have no idea what's going on but something is wrong. I need Phoenix. I squeeze Auntie Hattie's hand and she looks down at me. I whisper through pain and tears, "Phoenix." She tells me not to worry and that she will call him when we get to the hospital. We make it downstairs and out the double doors to a waiting ambulance. They load me into the back of the ambulance and we head to Kaiser Permanente. Auntie Hattie is in the back with me and she is on her phone calling the Highland Hospital trying to get connected to Phoenix's room. I cannot have these babies without Phoenix. Again, why is this happening to me? Phoenix is across the Bay in another hospital and I am on my way to another hospital and can't possibly be having our babies without him. It's way too early to deliver. I start praying that God spares their lives and allows them to survive. I pray that He also allows Phoenix to recover so that we will be able to raise these babies together. I am so overwhelmed right now and cannot withstand another tragedy. We make it the emergency room at Kaiser San Francisco and I hear someone scream, "Get her into maternity exam room one, now!" Once in the room, a nurse takes off my soiled sweats and underwear, and t-shirt. She covers my body with a blanket and tells me everything will be okay. Another nurse starts an IV in my arm when my doctor walks in. She quickly examines me and tells the nurse to get me prepped for an emergency C-section. "What's wrong Dr. Allen? I can't have these babies without Phoenix," I cry. She responds, "I have no choice, the babies are in distress. It appears that one of the twins has the cord around its neck and something else is causing the bleeding. I need to get the babies out now." I start crying even more now. Within seconds I'm wheeled into an operating room. Everyone is moving about quickly. I see out of the corner of my eyes that there are two incubators behind my doctor and there is a doctor and nurse on either side of them. Auntie Hattie walks in with another nurse. She comes up to the head of the bed and puts her cell phone up to my ear. "Baby, you can do this. I'll be right here with you the entire time. I need you to relax and do what the doctor tells you to do," Phoenix says. I can't respond because I am crying hysterically. Dr. Allen tells me she needs me to try and relax so that the anesthesiologist can administer the spinal block with bupivacaine to get started with the C-section. I try hard to comply and to hear Phoenix on the phone is helping me. The nurse tells Auntie Hattie that she will call Phoenix on the phone in the room so he can be on speaker. Auntie Hattie disconnects the call and gives the nurse the number. She tells her that he's at Highland recovering from an accident. The nurse says, "Okay, let's get the husband on the phone." These people work fast because suddenly all the pain I was feeling has disappeared. "Baby, can you hear me?" "Yes." "Good. Dr. Allen, can you please explain what is going on?" Dr. Allen gives him a breakdown of what's going to happen. She tells him that they have a full room with labor and delivery nurses as well as a neonatal intensive care (NICU) team and respiratory nurses. She indicates that there are two neonatologists standing by as well. "We are going to give Sydney a uterine lower segmented cut (cut at the bikini line) and retrieve the babies. We will work fast because Sydney has suffered an erupted placenta. She will not feel any pain, some pressure and tugging but not pain during the procedure." He acknowledges what Dr. Allen has told him and seems even more worried and hurting because he cannot be there for Sydney or to see his babies born. Phoenix asks his auntie to please video it with her cell phone. She agreed to do so and to give him a play by play as it unfolds. Dr. Allen shouts out some instructions and tells me, "Here we go Sydney, let's bring these babies into this world."

Chapter 12

Auntie Hattie starts to tell Phoenix what's going on. "Okay baby, the doctor is cutting Sydney now." "Sydney, baby I love you so much. You are doing great. Hang in there baby and very soon we will be parents to beautiful babies," he says. There is no response from Sydney. Auntie Hattie looks over at her and she is knocked out. Auntie Hattie tells Phoenix, "she's missing it too baby, she's sleep." Auntie Hattie then tells him how they are tugging at her stomach and he indicates he doesn't want to hear any more of the gory details and that he only wants to know how Sydney is doing and when the babies come out. Dr. Allen shouts, "Here we go!" as she pulls one of the babies out. "It's a girl!" She cuts the cord and hands the baby girl to a nurse. Auntie Hattie screams, "It's a girl, Phoenix!" "Auntie I can hear, I'm on speaker remember?" he replies. "Oh sorry, I got a little excited." A few minutes later Dr. Allen says, "Okay, here comes the second one. It's a boy!" She does the same; cuts the cord and hands the baby boy to a nurse. "It's a boy!" Auntie Hattie shouts again. "Oh, I'm sorry, you already know that because you can hear." "Auntie, what is going on? How are the babies? How is Sydney? I didn't hear them cry." Phoenix asks, concerned. Dr. Allen turns around, as she also seems concerned as well. The doctors and nurses are doing whatever it is they are supposed to do to get the babies breathing, moving, and crying. The room is quiet. Auntie Hattie tells Phoenix to hang on so they can tell us what is going on. Phoenix speaks a little louder over the speaker and to no one in particular, "I need someone to tell me what the hell is going on." Dr. Allen was about to speak when he heard what sounds like a faint cry. "Is that a cry? Are our babies crying?" A male voice says, "Yes. Baby girl just let out a cry." "What's happening with our baby boy?" "We're still working to get him breathing," a different voice responds. I guess the medication had me out because I'm waking up to hearing someone say our baby boy is not breathing. "Phoenix, what's happening?" I cry. "It's going to be okay baby. He's a fighter like us, he will pull through. They will both be okay baby. I need you to stay strong right now. Okay, can you do that for me?" "I don't know but I will try," I reply through tears. Auntie Hattie tells Phoenix that one team has left the room with the baby girl and just as they were leaving, the baby boy lets out a faint cry. Dr. Allen tells me that I'm all stitched up and they will be moving me to recovery shortly. But before they move me to recovery, a doctor will come in to assess me to see if they can remove my casts. I was happy to hear this, but I want to see and be with my babies. I want to hold them and smell them. "When can I see our babies?" Dr. Allen tells me that they are in the neonatal unit and I can see them in a few days when I have some strength. "I need you to get some rest, you just had major surgery. It will be at least 3 days before we let you go, so in the meantime your aunt can take some pictures for you and Phoenix. I will go and check on them now and bring a report of what's going on. Because the babies are premature, they will need to stay in the hospital and in the incubators until they are close to their normal birth weight and due date. They are still developing, so they will be here for the next couple of months. In the meantime, you and Phoenix need to think about what you're going to name your prince and princess," she says with a smile. "How much do they weigh?" I ask in a weak voice. Dr. Allen tells me that our baby boy weighs 2 lbs. and 4oz and baby girl weighs 2 lbs. even. I think to myself that they are really small and tears continue to fall down my cheeks but I have to remind myself that they are very early. Phoenix tells me to hang in there and that he will get them to transfer him to Kaiser as soon as possible. I respond with saying, "Please hurry, because I can't do this by myself." I lay in the recovery room trying hard to believe I am a mother and a mother of two children no less. Still in shock from all the other tomfoolery that's going on, this is just the icing on the cake, the straw that broke the camel's back, stick a fork in me…I'm done! You get it? This is just way too much for any one person to handle. I wish I could get up and see my babies. I want to make sure they are okay. I want to touch them, smell them. I want to make sure they have all their fingers and toes. I want to see if one looks like me and the other like Phoenix or if they both look like him or me. These thoughts are running through my head and I can't stop thinking the worst. I have to trust what Dr. Allen says about the survival rate of twins born at 29 weeks. That still doesn't remove the worry from my mind. I'll be patient and wait until Auntie Hattie comes back with a report of good news I pray. She also told me she would take some pictures with her cell phone so I can see them. The anticipation is killing me. This was not the way I'd envisioned having the twins. I knew it was a good chance that I would need to have a C-section and I had come to grips with that; however, not having Phoenix here to hold my legs or hand and plant soft kisses on my sweaty forehead just killed me. Reassuring me all will be okay, it's confirmed that things don't always turn out the way you want them to but turn out the way they're supposed to and that everything happens for a reason. I pray the babies, Phoenix and the others will be okay. Soon after I gave birth, a doctor that I have never seen before came in and introduced himself as Dr. Carter and tells me he is the doctor that is going to remove my casts. "Well that will surely make me happy," I tell him. He tells me he just wanted to introduce himself and he'll be back to check on me later to see when it is a good time to remove the casts. As he is exiting the recovery room, Auntie Hattie is walking in with a big smile across her face. By the smile she is wearing I'm going to assume that she is the bearer of good news. She walks up next to my bed and begins to tell me what is seemingly making her very happy. I know it has to do with the twins but I don't want to steal her thunder. She opens her mouth to speak when another doctor enters the room. "Is this Grand Central Station?" I ask. The female African-American doctor apologizes for the interruption after my statement. Her short, round, fluffy body reminds me of a female version of the Pillsbury Doughboy. I laugh to myself because she's cute but I just want to squeeze her to see if she makes the 'Whoo-Hoo' sound. I know it's wrong but it brought me joy for a very brief moment. Anyway, she introduces herself as Dr. Kimberly Sutter, the neonatal doctor assigned to the twins.

Dr. Sutter informs me that there will be a series of drugs administered to make sure their lungs develop fully. She also explains that they will need to have feeding tubes as well. They will need to stay in the hospital until they gain weight, which will be close to their delivery date, which is what Dr. Allen had mentioned. "So in other words, they will be here close to 55 days, pending all goes well," she says. She reassures me they will be okay and she believes they're fighters just like their mom and dad. I guess the look on my face asks, how she knows how much of a fighter Phoenix and I are. "I had a conversation with your aunt in the NICU unit and she explained to me what was going on," she explains. I let my face muscles relax. She hands Auntie Hattie her business card and tells us not to hesitate to contact her if we have any questions or concerns. Before she exits my room she tells me congratulations and our twins are beautiful. Auntie Hattie's excitement flares up again as she looks at her cell phone. "Got it!" she yells. She slides her finger across the iPhone button then enters her code to unlock the phone. I'm holding my breath; again the anticipation is killing me. Auntie Hattie finally gets to the pictures and says, "Sydney, meet your son." I take a deep breath, close my eyes and when I open them, that instant love I felt after he was born is confirmed. I stare at the most beautiful little boy ever. His skin the color of smooth melted caramel, and his eyes are shut but he has the longest eyelashes I've ever seen. He has the outline of where his eyebrows will grow and he has Phoenix's mouth and pouty lips. He has a head full of straight, jet black hair. I can tell he is going to be a handsome boy. I flip through a few more pictures admiring how beautiful he is and embracing the love in my heart I'm feeling. I slid to the right and the next photo brought back tears to my eyes. Our little girl is just as beautiful as her brother is. She too has caramel colored skin; however, she is slightly lighter and she looks likes she might have freckles like Phoenix. Her facial features are close to her brother's but of course hers are softer. Her hair is also jet-black and straight but not as thick as her brother's. I guess the old wives tales is true; when you have bad heart burn during pregnancy it means your baby (ies) will have a lot of hair. While staring at my baby girl's picture, Auntie Hattie's phone rings, removing her picture and replacing it with a picture of Phoenix and his cell number. Auntie Hattie gives me the okay to answer her phone and I slid my finger across the screen and place it to my ear to hear Phoenix's voice. As soon as I hear his voice, the tear floodgates start to pour again. I can tell Phoenix is emotional as well by the way his voice sounds.

"Baby, have you seen our beautiful babies yet? They are absolutely beautiful. You did such a wonderful job and I'm so proud of you. I can't thank you enough for making me the happiest man on earth!" He says with so much enthusiasm and between sniffles. "I feel the same way babe. I couldn't have done it without you. I just pray they will both be okay, they're so small." I reply. He then asks me to put him on speakerphone so he could speak to Auntie Hattie and I at the same time. I did as he asked. Auntie Hattie lets him know she can hear him. He begins to thank her for being there for the twins and me. He tells us that he made arrangements to be transferred to Kaiser. I'm thinking, he doesn't have Kaiser Insurance so how is he able to be transferred to a hospital that's not in his network. Then I think, neither is the county hospital he's at. When you have a crap load of money, you can pretty much do what you want for a price and I'm sure as long as it's safe to do so. He says that he will be transported by ambulance first thing in the morning and Ben and CoCo will be accompanying him in the transfer. I was so happy I could hardly contain my excitement. He also says that Dr. Coverton played a major part in making the transfer happen. I bet he did, I think to myself. Auntie Hattie and I look at each other in amazement and this puts a smile on both of our faces. "Baby, Dr. Coverton arranged for us to be moved to a private room so we can be together. He spoke with your doctor and got the approval that you are healthy enough to move from the post labor and delivery to a private room." Phoenix also tells us that he tried to get our babies moved next to us as well but was told that was completely out of the question which he knew it was but thought he'd ask anyway. He says that we will pick out their names when he gets here.

Chapter 13

Auntie Hattie starts to cry and I ask her what's wrong. Phoenix asks what's going on and I tell him that Auntie Hattie is crying. "Auntie, what's wrong," he asks. She begins with an apology because she didn't mean to bring a happy occasion down but she says she wishes that his mom, dad, and sister were here to see the beautiful babies and to meet me for I am now a part of their family. She tells Phoenix that even though the twins are preemies and still not fully developed, she can see that they look like him and his sister when they were born. "I'll have to show you their baby pictures Sydney and I'm sure you'll agree," she says. Auntie Hattie calls Phoenix's name, with no answer from him. I turn to look at the screen on the phone and the screen saver replaces his picture and phone number, indicating he is no longer on the phone. The call either dropped or he hung up…I'm not sure which it was. "I'll call him back," I say to Auntie Hattie but she tells me to give him some time before I call him back. Okay, that weird feeling came back, the one I felt when I heard her tell Phoenix he had to talk to me. I know this is an emotional time for him; he's been shot, he didn't get the chance to see his babies born, and I'm sure he's still grieving for his parents and twin sister. Shortly after the phone call with Phoenix, I am moved to our private room. Dr. Brown came back to see how I am feeling and informed me that he will remove my casts once I've settled in to my new room. After the doctor left, a heavy sleepiness fell on me. I close my eyes and pray I can get some rest. Right before Dr. Brown came in, Auntie Hattie said she was going to check on the twins again and bring us back some food because she didn't want me eating the bland hospital food. It felt like I slept for hours but when I check the time on my cell phone, only an hour had passed. Well that was the best hour of sleep I had in a long time. Auntie Hattie re-appears carrying bags of food from Boston Market. She enters the room and the aroma from the food instantly makes my stomach growl. "I have baked chicken, cream spinach, mashed potatoes, bread and butter, salad and beverages," she says. I am so hungry I could eat a horse. So needless to say, I ate everything she prepared on the plate for me. We laugh and agree how good the food is and that she is a better cook by a long shot. The food was good and it hit the spot at the moment. We are interrupted yet again by the hospital staff and I think to myself, a person really cannot get any rest in the hospital with all that is going on. The worker brought the extra bed for Phoenix's arrival. The room is set up for two patients so basically we are not sharing with a stranger but with each other. I'm not sure what I expected from a 'private room' or what the room would look like but it's a hospital room, not the honeymoon suite. The worker positioned the bed in the empty space next to me and then excused himself. Auntie Hattie says that she will go because it is getting late and she wants to check on the twins one last time before she leaves. I convince her to stay because I don't want to be by myself. She agrees to stay and says she'll see me in a few. When she left to check on the twins, I call the nurse to see if I can have someone come and assist with a wash down. I lift my arm and get a whiff of my pits that brought tears to my eyes. The nurse came in and I tried to talk her into letting me take a shower but she informs me that I can't just yet because of my stitches but she will give me a sponge bath and bring me a toothbrush and paste to brush my teeth. After she is done, I laugh to myself and say, "Boy I feel like a new woman and one that smells somewhat fresh." When Auntie Hattie got back from seeing the babies, she indicates she's going to shower and hop in the bed. The bathroom doors open and out steps Auntie Hattie all fresh and wearing some pajamas. I laugh as I look at her and she says, "What?" "I see you're prepared." "If you stay ready you don't have to get ready," she says with a smirk on her face. Okay, I thought as I'm laughing out loud. "I guess you've been listening to the Suga Free lyrics huh?" She hops in the bed and I reach over for the remote and hit the on switch. We watch reruns of Criminal Minds with that fine ass Shemar Moore until we both fall asleep. My sleep is broken with a nurse slightly shaking me to check my vitals and to draw more blood. "Are you kidding me?" I ask. She apologizes for waking me up but says she has to follow the doctor's orders. I look over to the bed next to me and Auntie Hattie is not there. I ask the nurse what time it is and she responds with, "3:00 am". "Where in the world did she go?" I whisper. "She stopped by the nurses' station to let us know she was going to check on the babies, said she couldn't sleep with your snoring," she says with a chuckle in her voice. "Wow, it must have been bad if she couldn't sleep," I reply. "Let's just say it took me a hard shake to wake you up because you were calling the hogs for real," she says now laughing out loud. "Oh, you have jokes," I respond, laughing myself. The nurse left and I went back to sleep. The next thing I know I am being awakened again with the next nurse during the shift change at 7:00 am. There's a slight knock on the door and then enters Dr. Allen. She exchanges pleasantries with Auntie Hattie and I, then dives right in to why she's there. "Sydney, what kind of power do you have to get a private room for you and your Phoenix," she asks laughing, fully knowing who is behind this whole situation. Auntie Hattie interjects and tells her it is all Phoenix's doing. "I know. I just want to give Sydney a hard time." She checks my incision, says all looks good and I'll be able to go in a few days as soon as my blood pressure goes down. "Should I be worried," I ask. She reassures me that all is fine and it's normal for my pressure to be up after major surgery. Dr. Allen stays for a few minutes longer and says she's going to check in on the babies and she'll see me in a few days when it's time for my release. It is truly Grand Central Station again, when Dr. Allen leaves, the lactating nurse comes in to see if I'm ready to start pumping. I have completely forgotten about breast-feeding. The nurse shows me some basic positions for feeding and wants to see if I'm producing any milk. She indicates that sometimes the body might not produce for whatever reason and in the event that happens, we'll need to go straight to formula. We begin the pumping procedure when she notices that my nipples are inverted. She reaches into her little bag of goodies and hands me these plastic suction cups. She instructs me to place the cups over my nipples and allow my bra to hold them in place. This will allow my nipples to poke out making it easy for the babies to latch on. Auntie Hattie retrieves my bra out of the bag in the closet so I can follow her instructions. Once I get the bra on, it's a little tight so

Auntie Hattie says she will purchase the right bra for me once Phoenix and the others get here and settled in.

Ben arrives around 10:00am and they place him down the hall from me. They actually discharged CoCo, she called to say she would visit later in the week either in the hospital or once I make it home. Phoenix will be here by noon. His injuries are a little more severe so they want to make sure he is good to move. Ben wheels himself into my room even though he is fussing that he can walk. He says he wants to check on me before he went to see the baby girl and baby boy as he calls them. Ben and Auntie Hattie (his mother) leave the room and I'm wondering how their relationship will change now that they have been reunited. I lay in the bed thinking of names for the babies. I come up with River and Reign. I'm not sure where these names came from but I like them and I'm sure I will need to convince Phoenix to agree with me. I drift off to sleep for a while and when I awake Phoenix is lying in the bed next to me sound asleep. Wow, I must have been dead to the world because I didn't hear him or anyone else for that matter enter or exit the room. I look over at Phoenix and think to myself how lucky I am to have finally found someone who truly loves me for me. He doesn't judge me but accepts me for the imperfect person I am. Lost in my own thoughts, I hear Phoenix ask, "What are you thinking about beautiful?" "You." "I hope it's all well," he says with a smile. "Absolutely!" I ask Phoenix how he feels and if he's in any pain. He dismisses my questions and begins to speak about the twins and how I'm feeling. He tells me he's having a hard time thinking about names because he needs to see them, touch them and maybe he will be able to come up with names. I've heard people naming their children once they've seen them and I hear they do this as a part of their religion. I guess it's just preference for Phoenix; he needs to see his babies then name them. I'll wait to see what he says before I spring my names on him. Ben and Auntie Hattie return and Ben cannot stop talking about his niece and nephew. We sit and talk, laugh, and eat for hours. Phoenix mentions he wants to see the twins before the shift change and hits the button that calls the nurse. The nurse responds on speaker asking how she can help. Phoenix tells her what he needs and she appears within seconds. When she enters the room, she offers to assist Phoenix in a wheelchair. He is not connected to a multitude of tubes as he was before at Highland Hospital. Phoenix gets comfortable in the wheelchair and is ready to exit the room to see his babies in person for the first time. There's a knock on the door and Phoenix tells whomever it is to enter. Detective Watson enters the room and greets everyone. He says he went to Highland to see him and was informed that he and Ben were moved here. He tells us he has an update on Rocky. Phoenix says, "It will need to wait because I'm on my way to see my babies." The detective offers to go with them to see the babies as well. When they leave the room, Ben says, "I hope they fry that bastard!" "Benjamin!" Auntie Hattie yells as if to say what Ben just conveyed was inappropriate. He looks at Auntie Hattie and says, "Yes, mother?" Whatever Auntie Hattie was going to say went right out the door when he calls her 'mother'; she is at a loss for words. There are a few moments of silence then we all break out in laughter. Auntie Hattie tells Ben she's going to knock his head off for being a smart-ass. I think to myself, I really need to call my sister and let her know what's going on but she and her husband are out of the country in Austria on vacation and I don't want to ruin their vacation and worry her. She will kill me though when she finds out all that has gone on and that her niece and nephew have arrived early.

Chapter 14

Ben exits the room, leaving Auntie Hattie and I alone. She asks if I have thought of any names for the babies. I tell her yes but didn't want to discuss them until Phoenix and I agree. An hour passes when Ben, Phoenix and Detective Watson return from seeing the babies. They are all smiles and Phoenix has tears in his eyes. He expresses to Auntie Hattie and I that they are two of the most beautiful babies he has ever seen. Phoenix then says to everyone to have a seat so we can pick and agree on names. Everyone has their own idea of what their names should be, and funny enough so does the detective. When did he become a part of the family? I think and laugh to myself. Auntie Hattie says she thinks their names should be Grace and Caleb. Ben comes up with Chloe and Zachary and Detective Watson adds Kimberly and Keagen. Phoenix tells them all the names suggested are beautiful but they don't seem to fit the twins. Ben yells, "Let's see what you came up with." Phoenix looks at me and says, "China and Zaire." Ben yells again, "You would pick names that are cities, states or countries. That's real original man." Everyone laughs and Phoenix tells Ben to shut up. "Baby, what are the names you came up with?" he asks me. "Well, I thought River and Rain, spelled R-e-i-g-n, would be nice." Everyone looks at each other, like they're contemplating the names. "I love them baby and I love the names I selected as well. How about we compromise and name them, China Reign and River Zaire Davenport?" Phoenix says with tears in his eyes. Auntie Hattie claps her hands and says, "That's it, it's settled. Our babies have been officially named." Phoenix and I are happy about the names and he seals our selection with a passionate kiss. Ben tells us to get a room and Phoenix responds with, "We have one and right now you're in it." We all laugh because these two are pure comedy.

I cannot wait for us to get out of here so we can start on the road to recovery and try to get back to some type of a normal life. Detective Watson clears his throat and brings me out of my thoughts and gets everyone's attention. He starts with, "Rocky is in protective custody because of death threats. He has been charged with three counts of kidnapping for (Phoenix, Ben, and Cameron); two counts of first degree murder (Cameron and Officer Becker); four attempted murder charges for (Phoenix, Ben, CoCo, and Officer Carter, who by the way made it out of surgery and will be ok); and a long list of other charges once we can tie him to masterminding the whole set up. Believe me, Rocky will be going up the river for a very long time. He will stay in protective custody at the county jail until the bail hearing then depending on the charges; he'll be moved at that time. "How do you know someone is trying to kill him?" Ben asks. The detective tells us that news travels fast in jails and prisons. It is also based on who the criminal is, what he did and whom he did it to. There are inmates waiting for the criminal's arrival who are friends, family members, or homies of the victims. They will have a chance to enact revenge on the new inmate to prove himself or make a name for himself or even repay a debt for another inmate. "There can be a list of other reasons. We really don't know the reason, however, I can think of a few but my opinion doesn't matter. The moment he arrived at the county jail, we got word he was a mark. I despise Rocky and can care less about what happens to him, but I still have to do my job and protect him. I want him to have his day in court for all he has done. I had to tell my fellow officer's wife and two children that her husband and their father was killed in the line of duty. This was the first and I pray the last time I ever have to make this kind of visit to my fellow officer's." Detective Watson expresses. I wonder if Justin has anything to do with the mark on Rocky's head. Justin is in the county jail for domestic violence so I would imagine Rocky might not be in the same part of the jail because of his crimes but then again I have no idea how any of that works. Justin is popular on the inside from what I understand and is respected by many, so word of Rocky's arrival could have spread like a wild fire.

Detective Watson picks up on the concerned look on my face and decides to offer some additional information. "Things happen in jail that need no explanation as to why or who did it. Sometimes you will have an inmate that is a real bad ass and pissed at another inmate for whatever reason. So, if the badass inmate has a problem with another inmate he can have a flunky, bunkmates or cellmates do his dirty work so it doesn't come back on him. They will send a 'kite', that's prison lingo for the word or a message, that this other inmate needs to be handled. Now understand the badass inmate could give the order or as I said a flunky, bunkmate, cellmate, etc. can take it upon himself and order a mark unbeknownst to the badass inmate. I hope I have explained this scenario so you can understand that there are times even though the bad ass inmate wants payback on someone who has wronged him, he might not be the one responsible for it happening." he explains. That makes perfectly good sense and I understand. As much as Justin would love to put his hands on Rocky, he wouldn't for the simple fact that he only has a few months left on his sentence and I would hope that he doesn't want any added charges or time. The last time I visited Justin, he told me he has been the model prisoner, keeping his nose clean so he can get out on schedule. Now, we all know that my brother has a horrible temper but this little vacation he's been on has helped him control his temper and he also realizes what's really important in life...us and his freedom. Phoenix calls my name to bring me out of my personal thoughts. "Yes?" "Do you think your brother has anything to do with the mark on Rocky's head?" he says. "No! Justin has nothing to do with this. You don't even know him, how dare you pass judgment on my brother and those words better never come out of your mouth again!" I scream. Phoenix doesn't reply. He just displays a look of regret on his face for asking the question. I think everyone in the room was also taken aback by my outburst as they display the same look on their faces. Hell, yes the thought crossed my mind but when Phoenix said it, it instantly changes my mood. I ask everyone to leave the room. I want to be by myself. I want to be left alone to get a handle over all of these thoughts that are flooding my head. Detective Watson is the first to stand, Auntie Hattie, and then Ben. Auntie Hattie gets behind Ben's wheelchair and they all exit the room. I feel really bad but I just need to be alone. When they leave and the door is closed behind them, Phoenix tells me he's so sorry for upsetting me and that he was not accusing Justin of any such acts, he was just asking a question. I say nothing, just lie back in the bed and turn my back to him. Phoenix pushes his bed closer to mine, gets in it and falls asleep. The next morning, the lactating nurse comes in to see if I can pump and save milk. I turn to say good morning to Phoenix and he's not there. The nurse mentions that he and another gentleman in a wheelchair said they were going to see the babies. Another nurse enters the room with a slight knock on the door and wearing a big smile. She tells me that she has good news and informs me that I will be discharged within the next 24 hours. "Whoo Hoo," I sing. After my vitals are checked, I pick up my cell phone that's charging on the table next to the bed. I dial CoCo's number. She answers on the second ring and is happy to hear from me. We catch up on how she's feeling and I let her know that we're being released in a few days. I tell her that I will get the key to my apartment to her because I want for her and her family to stay at the apartment. I lost my battle with Phoenix about not moving in so to compromise, I will keep my apartment and let CoCo and her family stay there. Phoenix and I fix up one of his spare bedrooms and make it the nursery so when the twins come home, their room will be fit for a prince and princess. But at first they'll stay in the master bedroom with us.

Chapter 15

Within the next few days Phoenix, Ben and I are released from the hospital. We are all trying to get settled in and back to a somewhat normal life. Phoenix and I spend every waking moment at the hospital. The twins are doing well, growing each day and we will soon be taking them home. They will need to gain enough weight and be able to digest their food. The doctor told us that it will be closer to their due date before they can come home. In the meantime, we're waiting for Rocky's hearing to determine when his trial will begin. I've tried to visit Justin but he is refusing my visits. I'm not sure why he won't see me but I need to know everything is alright. I need to make sure he is okay. If all goes well, he will be released around the same time the babies come home. Amber and her husband made it home from their vacation to learn they have a niece and nephew, and that Rocky is in jail for killing Cameron and an undercover cop. She was so angry that I didn't call her so she could have come home to help me through all this madness. I'm looking at her with the twins and she is truly happy for us. She cries when she looks at them and I think her tears are those of happiness and sadness because she has not been able to have her own children. When I bring up the subject of her maybe going to a fertility specialist she changes the subject. I told her that I did some research and she could be a candidate for an IVF procedure, but again she changes the subject. I'm sure when she's ready to talk she'll let me know. I didn't have a baby shower yet because the babies came early, so she feels like she has to bring bags and bags of clothes and toys every time she comes over. I call her and ask if she can meet me for some coffee to talk about some things on my mind. In an hour, we meet at Starbucks on California Street in San Francisco. I order our coffee and sit at a table facing the door eating a piece of Raspberry cake when she enters. She kisses me on the cheek and sits in the seat across from me. I have a knot in the pit of my stomach. I guess she can see that by the distressed look on my face. She reaches across the table, grabs my hands and asks what's wrong. "There are a few things on my mind I'd like to talk to you about." She sits back in her chair, takes a sip of her coffee and gives me her undivided attention. I start by telling her how I walked in on Auntie Hattie and Phoenix talking about how he needs to have a conversation with me about his past. I get no reaction from Amber, which is weird because she generally has a great deal to say. I wait a few seconds for a response then continue. "Should I confront him about knowing there's something he needs to tell me or should I just wait until he does. I'm afraid of what he might say or be hiding," I say. There's still no response from Amber. I'm seriously perplexed as to why my sister is not commenting on what I'm discussing with her. I begin to speak again when she cuts me off and says, "Sydney, don't speculate, assume, or draw your own conclusions. Phoenix is a good guy. We've all had issues in our lives and I'm sure he will talk to you when he is comfortable. I'm sure he's waiting for you and the twins to get stronger so it will be easier for you to process whatever it is he has to say." Wow, I think to myself, I just want to have a conversation with my sister and not a counseling session with Dr. Amber Marshall-Monroe. She's acting weird. What's going on with her? I think. "Amber, do you know something and you are keeping information from me?" I ask. She looks away which tells me she does know something yet no words exit her mouth. "You better not be hiding something from me and spill what you know right now!" I shout. Amber looks at me not fazed by my threat and says, "What else do you want to talk about?" Did she just ignore me and move on to another question I ask myself. This heffa is getting on my nerves. "Okay, since you don't want to spill the beans I guess I have no other choice but to move on." Still no response, just a blank stare so I choose to move on to my next subject...Rocky.

"I want to go visit Rocky." I explain to her that he owes me an explanation as to why his ass flipped out the way he did. It couldn't be because he so-call 'loves me'. It has to be another reason for his actions. I really think he's sick and probably bi-polar, manic depressant, or schizophrenic. This might be the only reason to explain his behavior of being a normal person one day and cold blood killer the next. Amber looks at me like I have two heads. "Have you lost your everlasting mind Sydney? That man tried to hurt you and did hurt people you love and care about. How can you possibly think it's okay to visit that maniac!?" she shouts. I try and explain that seeing him will help me with closure with regards to what happened. She tells me that I'll have closure when I see them stick the needle in his arm with a lethal injection. Well, I guess she has a point but I still have this strange need to see him. Amber goes on about Rocky for another 20 minutes then suggests we get going to the hospital to see the twins. We finish our coffee and head to the hospital to relieve Auntie Hattie and Phoenix. Amber and I visit the babies for 5 hours. River will have his first feeding without the feeding tube. I give Auntie Amber the pleasure of feeding him, still with the tube but now there is a little nipple on it, it reminds me of the little bottles that come with a baby doll. The good news is that the tube is not strapped down to the side of his cheek. Still in the incubator, she reaches through the hole in the front of the incubator and proceeds to feed him with the nurse giving her instructions along the way. It takes him a second to get it and latch on, then he starts to suck. I'm looking over my shoulder at her and him because I'm across the room with both my hands in the incubator rubbing the arm and leg of Reign. I pray for our babies' everyday that they are healthy and that they will be able to come home soon. After our visit, we head to the penthouse for a family dinner that Phoenix and Auntie Hattie are preparing. Auntie Hattie is fussing around in the kitchen making sure everything is in order and perfect for our meal. Ben has the formal dining room table set for 8. "Who all are we expecting?" I ask. "CoCo, your sister, her husband, me, mom, you and Phoenix. We even have room for any unexpected guests," Ben explains. When the rest of the guests arrive, we all hang out in the family room, talking, laughing, and sipping wine and brandy, waiting patiently for Auntie Hattie to let us know dinner is served. Auntie Hattie calls us to the table. Phoenix blesses the food and we begin to pass the dishes around filled with amazing food. She made a shrimp, lobster and crab scampi. We had our choice of either rice or pasta. There is a garden salad, French bread, grilled asparagus, garlic mashed potatoes, and prime rib cooked to perfection. When all you hear is forks clanking on plates and there is no conversation, you know that people are enjoying their food. Our silence is broken when Auntie Hattie asks Phoenix if he has talked to us about the memorial service for X. The mood suddenly changes but it's a conversation we need to have. "Phoenix and I spoke about it and he mentioned he would discuss the details with the others once we were all together," I respond. "Now that you brought it up Auntie, I guess there's no better time like the present," Phoenix says facetiously and gives his aunt a disappointed look. She ignores his look, comments and indicates that it is a good time to talk about it. Phoenix begins to tell us that according to X's family, he had instructions to be cremated. X had life insurance and his family is financially able to take care of any and all fees involved with the service. "I insisted that I take care of all the fees involved. X was one of my closest friends and I feel responsible for his death," Phoenix says with conviction in his voice. He tells us that the service is scheduled for the upcoming Tuesday and would hope that we all attend. There are remarks and agreements around the room. After we all agree to attend, there is an uncomfortable silence in the room. That silence is broken when Phoenix's cell phone rings. He places his lap napkin on the table and excuses himself. Auntie Hattie asks if we were done with dinner and ready for dessert. CoCo, Amber and I clear the table while the men head to the family room to relax after their bellies are full. Everyone refuses dessert for now, as they are too full, leaving the peach cobbler, vanilla bean ice cream and upside down 7-up cake to be devoured later.

115

Chapter 16

"I'm trying to get used to my current situation and more than likely my new permanent residence. I know that I fucked up but I've come to grips with it. What's done is done and I had to do what I thought was right to get the woman I love. Looks like that shit backfired. My attorney told me what charges I'm facing. I'm glad that punk ass Cameron is dead. I wish I popped a fatal bullet in Phoenix's ass too! The things you do for love. I'm no fool and know that Justin is aware that I'm here. He has a temper but I know he only has a few more months left so I'm sure he won't do anything stupid to jeopardize his release. I have to watch my back. I also know that we are on different levels. Justin is in for domestic violence and would be on level 1 or 2 whereas for my crimes, I'm on level 3 or 4," Rocky says out loud to himself. When I got off the bus and was processed, I was in the reception center, that's where all inmates are until they determine where to send us. While waiting in the reception center, a few inmates bump into me and tell me to watch my back. They make an announcement that we will be divided into several units and each until will have several tiers. I think again that I'll be protected because Justin is on a different level. If it comes down to it, I'm not a punk and I can handle my own and will step to anyone who steps to me. I'm from the streets of Richmond and I had my share of battles and this will be no different, he says. The word has already gone out to an inmate trustee (this is someone who is trusted to get a message to whomever) that something needs to go down. Even though Justin and Rocky are divided, there are several opportunities for their paths to cross and unfortunately this is unknown to Rocky. For breakfast, all levels and units line up at one time. Each level (tier) has 20 minutes to finish their meals and exit before the next unit is ushered in. This morning halfway through breakfast Rocky spots Justin but Justin is leaving out and Rocky is coming in the chow hall. There is a sigh of relief that Rocky has because he doesn't have to face Justin, well at least for now. Rocky is so focused on Justin that he doesn't see a fist coming straight for his face. This giant white guy with tattoos and a shaved head draws back and punches Rocky smack dab in the nose, breaking it. Rocky falls to the floor and blood is squirting everywhere. He is so taken aback because he didn't see it coming nor who hit him because it happened so fast. A guard rushes to his aid while the rest of the inmates keep on with their routine. The guard helps Rocky off the floor and accompanies him to the infirmary to seek medical attention. Once Rocky is in the custody of the doctor, the doctor tells him he'll be right with him as he was tending to another inmate who looks like he's getting some type of injection. The doctor then tells Rocky and the other inmate that he will be right back. He walks out of the office to answer the phone in the other office. When he leaves, the other inmate opens some drawers and stuffs some things in his pockets. The guard is looking the other way and sees nothing and neither does Rocky. Another inmate is brought in also with a bloody broken nose. The guard starts talking to the other guard as they wait for the doctor to re-enter the clinic. The doctor ends his call and returns to the clinic releasing the inmate he had administered the injection to and tells the new inmate that he will be right with him then turns his attention to Rocky. He cleans up the blood from

117

around his nose and notices that he has a two-inch gash that needs stitches. He gave Rocky the stitches, two painkillers and sends him on his way. The doctor then assists the other inmate that came in with a bloody nose as well. Rocky has a feeling something is strange and whatever the other inmates have planned for him will have to wait until another time because he's sure they didn't expect the guards to stick around.

Phoenix, Auntie Hattie, Ben, my sister, her husband, CoCo and I all pile in a small chapel on Tuesday morning to say our last goodbyes to X. He has a large family in the sense of size and family members; it's the Samoan culture I think. Anyway, X wanted to be cremated so his family did follow his wishes even though his mother insisted that he be buried. He has 16 nieces and nephews ranging in age from 4 to 19. They all sang a beautiful song in his honor. It was so touching and you knew they all loved and respected their uncle. X was never married and had no children. Maybe he thought there was no need to have them because he already had a team of nieces and nephews...I chuckle to myself cause I can hear him saying, "I don't need no damn kids." X was very loved; all of the friends and family that spoke had nothing but good things to say about him. I thought to myself, "Will anyone ever have the nerve to get up at a funeral and just totally bash the dead?" I remember when I first met him. I wanted to smack the shit out of him because he had a smart-ass mouth and wouldn't do what I wanted him to do. He told me he didn't work for me but worked for Phoenix and took his orders from him. To know X is to love him. Phoenix is really taking this hard, they were really good friends and regardless of what we say regarding his death, he still feels responsible. I heard from some friends that Cameron's services would be held later this week and CoCo was told that his family requested that we not attend. They said they would love to be able to send their loved one away in peace and not with the circus of the media or the people who got him killed. You heard me; his family is blaming us for his death. I guess they forgot that Cameron was a live wire and that he stayed in the media for something or another but we had him killed...Okay whatever. I also heard that his family is filing a suit against the Oakland Police Department for setting him up in the first place. Detective Watson told us not to worry about it because Cameron was the one who asked for the meeting with him and I. This is too much and I can't wait until all of this madness is over. After we leave the service, we head to the hospital to spend some time with the babies before heading home. I notice that Ben and CoCo are getting close. I saw him comforting her during the service and holding her hand as we left. It could be nothing but I will surely ask. After spending time with the babies, Phoenix and I are lying in bed watching the news when they mention the service for X and speak on the upcoming service for Cameron and the fallen officer, which will have full media coverage. My mind keeps drifting back to the conversation I walked in on Auntie Hattie and Phoenix. I want to bring it up but I don't think he knows I heard them talking. It's killing me because I love this man and if we are going to be together, I need to know all about him so I can make an informed decision if I want to stay with him or not. Okay, I might be taking it a bit too far due to my life being a hot mess and he fell in love with me for who I am and didn't care about my past. I would have to say that unless he tells me he is a mass murderer, then all bets are off. My cell phone rings. I reach to pick it up off the nightstand and answer it. I look at the caller I.D. and was happy to see, Oakland County Correctional Facility display across the screen of my iPhone. Finally Justin is calling, I think. I quickly slide my finger across the screen to answer the phone when I hear the recording, "Do you accept a collect call from an OCCF inmate, please say yes or press one." "Justin, it's about time you called me." "Oh baby, this is not Justin. This is the man that would kill for you, hell that did kill for you. Sydney I know you love me, you're just playing hard to get but I need you to listen to me and listen good. You need to be at my hearing ready to post bail for me. I know you have the money and you know where I stash mine. Make sure my sister gets my stash and be ready to apologize to me for making me do all these things for you. You gave me no choice. I had to get the people out of the way so we could be together," Rocky says. A recording comes across the line indicating that there is only a minute left on the call. I interrupt Rocky about to speak again, "You sick son of a bitch, your ass will rot in jail before I ever do anything to help you! And unless you are feeding me, financing me or fucking me, you don't tell me what the fuck to do!" Before he could get another word out, the call disconnects. Phoenix looks at me and says, "Don't accept anymore calls." I tell him I have to because Justin might call and I need to talk to him to make sure he's okay and I need to know why he's not taking my visits. "I need to know my brother is okay. I don't want him to do anything stupid to Rocky because he only has a few

120

more months and I need him home. As a matter of fact, I know he won't do anything stupid because he wants to come home. He wants to be a better person. He told me this the last time I saw him so I'm not going to worry. He'll be fine and he will keep his nose clean."

Chapter 17

Phoenix tells me not to worry and pulls me closer to him. As I lay in his arms, which seems like it's been forever, I feel comfortable and safe. Phoenix plants soft kisses on the side of my face. His breathing is getting heavy. I close my eyes because at the moment his lips feel so good and I'm so horny. Neither one of us is in any condition for some hanky panky, but Phoenix tells me he needs to taste me. I know we both need to settle down, but I allow him to slide between my legs and give me what I call the 'triple dipper'. His tongue flickers across my clit, his finger is inside me stroking my G-spot and his thumb penetrates my ass, oh what a feeling! He gets me there with a quickness and it's just what I need. I tell him to scoot up close to my face so I can return the gesture; I want to feel him swell in my mouth. He denies my request and we continue to watch T.V. in each other's arms until we fall asleep. I hate when he denies me the pleasure of pleasing him. The next time I won't ask, I'll take what I want. We wake up in the morning to the smell of food. We both shower and throw on some clothes and head to the kitchen. When we reach the kitchen, Auntie Hattie, Ben and Detective Watson are sitting at the kitchen table. "Good morning sleepy heads," Auntie Hattie says to us when we enter the kitchen. The others say good morning as well and Phoenix asks the detective what was the reason for his early morning visit. Detective Watson tells us that the preliminary hearing is scheduled. He also tells us that the case is getting a great amount of publicity and they want to move the trial to a different county. He says, "It doesn't matter where the trial is, Rocky will not get off. He killed a cop and Cameron. He has a long laundry list of other charges. He has a number of witnesses, which will make this an open and shut case. Rocky will get what's coming to him, hopefully the death penalty." He goes on to tell us that his attorney had the nerve to say that it was a crime of passion. "That will not fly. It was pure pre-meditated murder. We followed all the rules and didn't cut any corners so they can't throw anything out on technicalities. Everything was by the book," Detective Watson says. Phoenix indicates that Rocky is still causing trouble as he called last night and Phoenix told the detective what he said. Ben asks that we change the subject and starts to speak about how he is in love with River and Reign and cannot wait for them to come home to Uncle Ben. We all fall out in laughter and Ben is wondering why. "What the hell is so funny," he asks. Phoenix, still laughing, says, "Uncle Ben?" Ben finally gets in and joins in on the laughter. Phoenix and I leave the house and head to the hospital. On the way there, I start a conversation and I'm thinking of a way to possibly have him tell me whatever it is he needs to tell me. I'm just afraid of what it is and when you know someone has something to tell you, it will eat you alive until you find out what it is. I don't want to taint my image of him but I keep reminding myself that we can start over every day. Thank God we all have second chances and we all have the ability to change and be who we want to be. We also have the ability to leave the past behind and learn from our mistakes and move on. The bottom line is we decide our own destiny and it's never too late to change. As these words leave my thoughts, Phoenix grabs my hand and says to me that he knows he needs to talk to me about some things and he will, he just feels now is not the best time to do so. He reassures me that it's nothing for me to worry about and that as soon as our family is back in order, we will sit down and talk and he will let me know everything there is to know. I have no idea how long it will take for our family to 'be back in order' I think to myself, but continue to look out the window and simply respond, "Okay." I'm also thinking the thought of visiting Rocky is clearly not a good idea due to the call I got last night. He's still really crazy and he will not understand the reason for my visit. I'm sure he will confuse my visit as feeling the same way he does and Lord knows that is not the case. I don't want to confuse him no more than he already is. We get to the hospital and make our way to the NICU unit and to our surprise Dr. Coverton is there. Why is he here, I think? This is not his hospital to cover so why the hell is he here. Phoenix gave him the Bro hug and dap then thanks him for all the stops he pulled to get him to Kaiser. Brandon turns to me and gives me a hug and tells me how good it is to see me and that motherhood does me right. I tell him thank you and leave to see the twins. He and Phoenix continue to chat it up for a little while longer. I get a report from the nurse that the twins are doing well and progressing as they should. I'm so uneasy to have my ex and my current chatting it up like they're old buddies. I'm almost certain that Phoenix doesn't know that Brandon and I used to be an item. I told myself that I was going to be honest in this relationship since it seems like it's the real thing so far and I don't want anything to mess that up. I don't want any secrets. He did just tell me that we will talk and I trust that all will be okay and he will let me in on his secrets as well. I just hate that I'm the only one in the dark, "Okay let it go Sydney," I say to myself. I look out the glass window and Brandon and Phoenix are laughing and talking like they've known each other forever. This cannot be good I think. What is Brandon up to? Why is he being so nice and going above and beyond the call of duty with Phoenix? I will have to tell Phoenix sooner than later about Brandon before whatever this is gets out of control. Phoenix makes his way in to see the twins. I turn to see Brandon standing outside the window and giving me that look I know so well. I excuse myself to go and speak to Brandon. Through clenched teeth I ask, "What the hell are you doing? What are you up to? Why the hell are you still around? You have gone above the call of duty to help us so you can leave now and tend to your other patients." Brandon gives me that sexy, evil smile and says, "I'm just following up on my patients. I got here to find that you guys were discharged so I came by to see the babies, and here you are. I just wanted to make sure my patient was healing properly. Is that a crime?" "No asshole, it's not a crime but your sneaky ass is up to something," I tell him. He responds by telling me I'm being paranoid and I need to learn how to relax. "Everything happens for a reason and people are placed in others lives for a reason and for a season. We had our season, now I'm here for a reason," he says as he starts to walk away. In mid-stride he stops, turns around and says, "By the way, Phoenix invited me to dinner." This pompous ass smiles, turns then proceeds to walk away. "What the fuck?" I say out loud. Phoenix and I stay at the hospital a few more hours before heading home. When we get in the car, Phoenix mentions that Dr.

Coverton is a nice guy and that he likes him. "This cannot be happening," I think to myself. I tell Phoenix that there is something I need to tell him. He cuts me off and expresses that everyone has a past and he cannot get upset about something that happened BP...Before Phoenix. "I saw the way he looked at you and knew you two had a past. I'm cool with it babe. We're together now and I love you with all my heart so that's all that matters. Plus, I informed Dr. Coverton that I knew you two had a past and wasn't sure what his intentions were but he needed to know that I'm not to be played with and if he was about some bullshit he'd better put it in his pocket and keep it pushing because I'm not the one. So don't worry baby, we have an understanding," he says. He then says, "Baby you really have the power of the 'P' because the brother's got it bad." We both laugh but my laugh is an uncomfortable one because I know Brandon will not go away that easy. Don't get me wrong he's not crazy like Rocky or at least I don't think he is, however, he is a master manipulator.

A month passes and we are getting ready for Rocky's hearing. We all sit together in the courtroom and Detective Watson joins us. When we entered the courtroom, Keisha (Rocky's ghetto-ass sister) stands up, points her finger at me and shouts, "This is all that bitch's fault. She's the reason my brotha is in jail. The first chance I get, Imma tap dat ass...bitch! You betta watch yo back." The judge hits his gavel to bring some order in his courtroom but when you have a bunch of unruly fools in one place it might be hard to do. "Young lady, I will have no more outbursts or threats in my courtroom. If I do, I will throw 'yo ass in da jail wit yo brotha' understood?" The courtroom burst out in laughter because the judge is clearly making fun of the way Keisha is talking. "Do you understand me," he asks again. "Yeah," she replies. "The correct response is, "Yes, Your Honor. Now take a seat and I don't want to hear a peep out of you." He looks at her, waiting for her to respond. She finally says, "Yes, Yo Honor," and takes her seat. Rocky comes in the courtroom in his orange jumpsuit with his hands and feet shackled. He scans the courtroom and makes eye contact with me. He then mouths the words, "I love you Sydney." I turn my head, as I can't stand to look at him right now. I can't even believe I wanted to go see his crazy ass. I'm glad I didn't, as I'm sure I would have regretted it. The judge denies bail for Rocky. The prosecutor and the public defender both spit out some words to the judge. The judge then asks Rocky to stand and tell him how he wants to plea. Rocky responds by saying, "Guilty." The courtroom erupts with gasps and cries. The judge then asks Rocky if he understands the charges and his rights and that he must testify under oath to facts establishing his guilt. Rocky shouts out he loves me and he did it for me. Keisha screams out, "This is some bullshit, she's got my brotha's head all fucked up." The judge hits his gavel again and tells Keisha that he warned her and asks the bailiff to remove her from his courtroom.

Chapter 18

The courtroom is in an uproar. The judge is irritated with all the interruptions with Keisha and Rocky. He tells the jailers to also remove Rocky. Once Rocky is out the room, he tells the court that the date for sentencing is scheduled for 2 months from now. He wants to move forward as quickly as possible due to the circumstances involving the case. I lean over to Phoenix and whisper, "That will be good because our babies and Justin should be home by then." Everyone is trying to get back to their normal lives. It's interesting that Ben and CoCo are still getting close if you know what I mean. Neither one has said anything to anyone but we are all taking notice as to how comfortable they're getting. Laughing with each other, getting very touchy feely, and I've noticed the long gazing stares. It's funny how tragedy brings people close together. Auntie Hattie mentions that Ben told her he took CoCo out to dinner. I don't think she thought anything of it but they have been spending time alone. I think it's confirmed they are feeling each other and possibly dating. Speak up people and let us know. Y'all could have been together long ago. I guess it's better late than never. They're actually really cute together and I pray it works out because they both deserve to be happy. The only sad part is that Ben doesn't have any kids and with Coco's recent hysterectomy she won't be able to have any more. She has two and their daddy ain't shit. Ben would be an excellent father; he loves kids. They're young enough to get adjusted to a man in her life. Auntie Hattie is so excited to have Ben in her life. They are developing their relationship now on a different level. Ben explains to her that he loves his parents and that will never change but now he has two moms. She's fine with that and completely understands. He's been in her life for the past 10 years but it's different now that he knows she's his biological mother. Ben now calls Auntie Hattie 'mom' and she lights up like a bulb when he does and when she calls him 'son', it has a whole different meaning. It will make her happy as well to see him happy and in a relationship.

Phoenix and I decide to go out to dinner. He says we need some alone time and wants to talk to me. I'm so excited because since all the drama we really haven't had much time together. It's always with the group and that's fine that we are a little clingy, hell we all pretty much almost got killed, so I get it. But in order for us to move on we have to try and get back to our normal routine, which was not spending almost every waking moment together. We ride to the restaurant in silence. I look out the window and admire the night's sky. Phoenix has the sunroof open and it's a little chilly. He sees me pull my jacket tighter and asks if I'm cold. "Just a little, but it feels good." He closes it halfway then turns on the heater and seat warmer. I'm super afraid of what he wants to talk about but ready for whatever. It's been killing me not knowing; now I'm scared shitless. Like I said, as long as he's not a psychopath, or a serial killer, I can deal with anything. This man loves me with all my flaws and I will love him with all of his...I hope. The least I can do is not judge him. Phoenix is quiet and I can tell he's nervous. He has pulled out all the stops once again. The restaurant is empty except for us, the serving staff, and a band playing soft music, coming from the back of the room. It's dimly lit with candles surrounding the room. It's a bit of the norm for Phoenix but romantic nonetheless and I'm appreciative of whatever this man does for me. I reach across the table and grab his hands letting him know it was okay and that he can be comfortable with telling me anything. He nods his head and tears start to form in his eyes. "Sydney, I know you say you will not judge me or feel differently about me but somehow I'm not sure you will once I say what I have to say," he confesses. "Okay Phoenix, you're scaring me, just come out with it already," I respond with frustration. Phoenix swallows hard and begins to speak. "In high school, my sister and I graduated at 16. We were skipped a few times which made us smart but I still lacked in social skills. Not being too mature, I started hanging with the wrong crowd. As you know, we come from money but kids with money at their disposal tend to get into more trouble. We're at a better advantage to get and do whatever we want. Even though I was hanging out with the wrong crowd, I still kept up my grades as I was attending Berkeley at the time. My father was hard on my sister and me because he wanted us to succeed. After a year at Berkeley, still getting into trouble and hanging with the local gangsters and drug dealers, my father saw that I could be really heading in the wrong direction and decided it was best for me to attend college out of the country. I got accepted to Oxford and off to the UK I went. When I completed my studies, I came back home and Ben moved to San Francisco with me. At the age of 20, all I wanted to do was party and hang out with my friends. My sister completed her studies at Stanford. She was a little more focused than me but I loved my sister with all my heart and she was my best friend. We shared everything and she generally was able to keep me on

130

track. Once we graduated, my father had plans for us to take over the company. He indicated he wanted me to be CEO and my sister CFO. My degree was in business and hers in economics so it only made sense to the direction he wanted us to go in. Like I said, she was more focused and I, well it took me a little longer to adapt to what my father wanted from me. I felt he was harder on me and didn't give me a break. I had the feeling that I let my father down and was turning into a big disappointment to him. So to deal with the stress, I started to do drugs to deal with my incompetence and inadequacies. At first, it was just a little coke to keep me up and focused, then it became more and eventually I couldn't go a day without it. The coke turned into crack and crack turned into heroin. I was a fast moving train going nowhere and I plummeted fast. Not caring about anything or anyone, I went off the deep end. Ben tried to help me on his own and when he couldn't control me, he contacted my parents. Of course I called him a snitch for ratting on me and I was so mad at him I cut all ties with him and my family. I was off the grid for 6 months and it tore my family apart not knowing where I was and if I was okay. My father cut off all my funds, cancelled my bank accounts and credit cards with the hopes of me coming home. It was bad Sydney. I did whatever I needed to do for my next hit. I ate out of garbage cans, I really hit rock bottom. A family member saw me destitute on the streets of San Francisco and called my parents with my current location. My parents and sister set out to rescue me and on the way to do that, they were killed by a drunk driver," he expresses. I am stunned and can't believe what I'm hearing. Phoenix continues, "Even though I was not responsible for that asshole that got behind the wheel of a car with a blood alcohol level 4 times the legal limit, I was on drugs which didn't make me any better than him but just as responsible for the deaths of my family. And to top it off, he walked away with not a scratch; however, he will spend the rest of his life in prison. This has been eating me alive ever since. I quit drugs and will never do them again. I can't allow anything or anyone to take my family away from me or to cause them harm. I was at a very weak point in my life and I want you to know that I'm not that man anymore and I will never be that man again. Baby you, our babies, Auntie Hattie and Ben are all I have and I will give my life to keep you all safe. Please don't hate me for not telling you this earlier but I was embarrassed and ashamed. I'm not perfect baby you know that and you know that no one is. I was lost for a brief moment and unfortunately the brief moment caused me to lose my family, the only people who meant the world to me. I never got a chance to redeem myself. I never got the chance to ask for their forgiveness. The last image they had of me before they died was that I was drugged out and eating out of trash cans. I wanted to kill myself. I didn't deserve to live after all I had put them through. Thank God for my Aunt, if it wasn't for her…I would be dead. I understand that hurt gathers over time. I've dealt with blow after blow, disappointment after disappointment, painful hit after painful hit and even though I know exactly how I got there it didn't mean I couldn't fix it. I can't heal every wound or fix what's broken and I'm okay with that but just because it's broken doesn't mean it needs to be fixed. Auntie Hattie told me that once she was watching a T.V. program and one of the actors said "It's painful to rip off the bandage because we don't want to see what's underneath, it might not be for the fear of the pain that holds us back, it might be because we're afraid to see if the wound is still open or if it might actually be healing." This spoke volumes to my life as much as it did to hers. Baby, I sit here before you with my heart on the outside of my chest. I forgave myself, which has allowed me to try and move on. I'm free from the guilt. I'll still have the pain because my family is not here but I'm not on my knees anymore not being able to look up. I'm able to stand on my feet and look everything and everyone eye to eye. This is the person I am and I'm giving you one hundred percent of me, the real me," he explains.

Chapter 19

Wow, I was not expecting this and I'm speechless. I have tears in my eyes and I cannot imagine how he must of felt having to deal with tragedy. Not to make this about me but we are really made for each other. It's interesting how having money doesn't remove the fact that we all can be fucked up. My heart goes out to Phoenix and I'm not at all upset that he didn't tell me earlier, in fact I love him even more because he has just spilled out his heart to me about the demons he's been dealing/dealt with and that makes me respect him more. I don't have pity or sorrow for him but I have nothing but admiration for him. I don't respond. I just hold his hands until I can remove the lump in my throat. I don't want to misspeak; say the wrong thing, so I remain quiet until I have the right words. Phoenix breaks the silence and says, "I'll need to get on my knees and look up to you," he says with tears in his eyes. He lets my hands go, pushes his chair back, comes over to my side of the table, kneels down on one knee and says, "Sydney Denise Marshall, I know I just dropped a lot on you and I hope it didn't damage the image and perception you have of me. We've been through a lot and have been together for little less than a year. Regardless to the short period of time that we've been together, I have fallen madly in love with you. I knew you were special from the moment Ben brought me to the club. I didn't care that you were a dancer. I knew what you did for a living but I saw beyond that, way beyond that. I saw a woman who was looking for love just as I was and I believe it was fate that brought us together. You have given me the best life has to offer...yourself, and our beautiful babies. I can't imagine my life without the three of you. I know this is a great deal to process and if you need some time to think about all of this, I totally understand, but know it will make me the happiest man alive if you would marry me." He is so emotional and so am I. I have been waiting for this day forever and yet I don't know how to respond. I'm happy, don't get me wrong but I really want this to be real and not some sick joke or bad nightmare. I want this to be real. My heart has been broken into so many little pieces that I can't afford for it to be broken down anymore. Somehow I believe Phoenix, I believe his love is true and the way I feel for him is the same but I want to make sure they're not just feelings and we're not just caught up in whatever this is. I want to know that without a shadow of doubt...that it's real. He then retrieves a black velvet box from his pant pocket, opens it and I promise you it seems like every light in the world lit up the restaurant. 'Shine bright like a diamond' is an understatement. Phoenix presents me with an 8-carat flawless, Gia pink platinum ring. My mouth drops open because I have never seen something so beautiful in my life. He stands, grabs my hand and I stand so we can look at each other face to face. Tears are rolling down my face. He takes his finger and wipes away tears and says, "I love you woman." "I love you too," I manage to say. He takes my left hand, slides the ring on my ring finger and says to me, "If you'll take me, I'd love to be your husband." "Yes, Phoenix I will marry you." We seal the moment with a passionate kiss that sends shock waves through my body. I need to have him right now. I tell him to make the staff disappear for a moment and he does as I ask. I walk over to him and unbuckle his pants. He grabs my hand and tells me we have time for this later. I ignore his plea. I get his pants down far enough that his erect package is visible, staring at me, waiting to feel my mouth and tongue. I get down on my knees and put him in mouth. I get Phoenix where he needs to be, pure bliss. I then pull my dress up and move my panties to the side. I sit on his lap and we ride each other. Damn, this man feels so good and he makes me feel like I have never felt before. We are a perfect fit. He fits perfectly inside me and knows what to do and how to do it and it drives me crazy. I was about to cum when I look up and see one of the servers taking in my little performance. I can see the lust in his eyes and I'm sure he is wishing he could ride this pussy next. Sorry mister, this pussy belongs to one man now and forever. He stares at me until Phoenix and I reach the ultimate climax. After our little fuck session, we both collect ourselves and finally have dinner. We sip champagne and bask in the moment. I can't wait to tell everyone our good news. On the way home, I call Amber. She answers on the second ring, singing 'hello' through the receiver. "Hey sis, whatcha doing?" "Hey girly. Nothing, just reviewing some case files for some patients," she replies.

I tell Amber I have some wonderful news and she starts screaming in the other end. I can't even get it out because she's screaming so loud. "Amber, calm down and stop screaming. I can't hear myself talk. Once you settle down, I tell you," I say. "What is it?" she says, still screaming. "I want you to know that Phoenix asked me to marry him tonight and I said yes." She's screaming again this time to her husband telling him that we are getting married. "I'm so happy for you sis. You deserve to be happy and now you will. You will have the whole package, the husband and the kids. Did you two talk about anything else?" she asks. Now she's fishing. "You already know what he wanted to talk to me about so why wouldn't you just tell me?" I ask. "Doctor-patient confidentiality, I couldn't," she responds. "What!? Are you fucking kidding me!?" I scream. She tells me not to get my panties all in a bunch and she'd been seeing Phoenix after I got hit by the car months ago. She explains that it was his wish not to say anything until he was ready and she had to respect that. She tells me not to be upset and to be patient with Phoenix because he's a good guy and has issues like all of us but he's working through them. I'm surprised and hurt that he went to her instead of me but I guess because she's the professional, I suppose. I hang up the phone with Amber and Phoenix grabs my hand and tells me not to be upset. We get home and on the ride up the elevator, Phoenix tells me he's knows I'm upset but asks that I forgive him for not telling me that too. He says we're celebrating our engagement and he wants me to be happy. When we reach the 18th floor, I step off the elevator not saying a word. The door is unlocked and I walk in with Phoenix in tow. When we enter the penthouse, we hear "Surprise!" Everyone is at the house even Amber and Kyle. Wow, she played that off as well. Everyone around me is feeding me a web of lies, I think. Okay Sydney, put on a happy face since your friends and family are here to celebrate your engagement, I say to myself. Everyone is hugging us and congratulating us. I look at Phoenix and say, "You were so sure I would say yes?" I ask. "I prayed you would," he says with the biggest smile on his face. He tries to hug me and I

137

jokingly push him away. Ben hands us a glass of champagne so we all can make a toast. We're all sitting in the family room just talking and laughing when Amber says she has something to talk to all of us about. She now has our undivided attention, then tells us that she and Kyle are ready to start a family and they will have to do fertility treatments. She explains that Kyle had cancer when he was young and the chemo treatments caused Azoospermia (a complete absence of sperm). His parents were upset that his doctor didn't suggest for him to store his sperm before his treatments but claimed they didn't know about it. "Well there's no need crying over spilled milk," Kyle says. He also tells us that Amber was smart to store her eggs some years ago due to the issues she has as well. He continues to say that they will do IVF (in vitro fertilization). Amber explains that because she's getting up there in age, her doctor wants to go aggressive and wants to start with her next cycle in a couple of weeks. "With that being said, I know we're celebrating Phoenix and Syd's engagement but we need to know if we can count on all you for support during this process," Amber asks. "We will need to select a sperm donor which brings me to the next part. Both Kyle and I are totally fine with this. We will need to pick a donor quickly, actually by next week. In order to make my next cycle, I've already started taking the drugs. Just so you know, they might make me emotional, evil or bitchy," Amber explains. I tell her "you mean more than you already are? Oh hell no, we don't need that," I say while laughing as did all the others. She tells me to shut up and continues with her instructions. Amber explains she will also need our help selecting the donor. Everyone is on board and happy to be a part of this process and the selection process as well. Auntie Hattie says, "Let's get this party started! There's no time like the present since we're all here now." Everyone agrees. Kyle retrieves his laptop from his bag and Phoenix provides the rest of the group with two additional laptops. Amber gives us the information to log onto the sperm bank's website. Apparently, she's already registered with the bank, which she tells us is the largest sperm bank in the country that's based in Los Angeles. They've been in business more than 35 years and came highly recommended by her fertility specialist. She provides us with her login and password as we all log on to the site. She then tells us what type of features she and Kyle are looking for. I notice the sperm bank has more than 500 donors available on their catalog. The website is pretty easy to navigate and it's pretty cool because you can see baby or childhood photos, their medical history is provided, their essays, personality assessments, and audio conversations, plus a number of other materials to help in the selection process.

Chapter 20

Auntie Hattie asks about adult photos because she didn't see any. Kyle explains that once we narrow down the selection they will send in his photo and a matching counselor will compare his features with that of the adult photo of the donor and let them know who has the best physical match. He also explains that with genetics nothing is guaranteed but they will get as close as they can and if their selections are not good they can either submit another group of donors or they can take his pictures and go through the database and select for them. "Thanks for that explanation Kyle. Okay, let's get started," Auntie Hattie says. "Kyle is Swedish, English, French and Italian. We're basically looking for a donor with this background; however, we can have a Caucasian donor with a similar background. He can have brown or blond hair (straight, wavy or curly hair); blue, green or hazel eyes. It really doesn't matter because my eyes are brown and will probably dominate. Anyway, we want him 6'0 or taller and the weight proportion to the height. As you can see, my baby has fair skin, so fair, medium or dark skin will work, again I'm sure my skin color will dominate," Amber tells us. "Damn, this is some cool shit, we're about to make a designer baby. Thanks for including me in this process Amber and Kyle, I'm honored," CoCo says with excitement in her voice. "You're family, so we're honored," Amber replies. She continues with telling us that the donor's education, sports, skills, and interests are not that important because they believe these things are more nature vs. nurture. However, she does mention that the medical history is very important. They want no mental illness, no cancers, or drug and alcohol abuse in the family background if possible. She knows that no one has a perfect medical history but they would like to get as close to one as possible. We all have our instructions and we break up into three groups. Kyle and Amber are in one group then Ben and Phoenix and last me, CoCo and Auntie Hattie. We all find that the website makes the search process easy because you can plug in all the information she gave us and it provides us with all the donors with those basic features. Phoenix asks if blood types are important and does it matter if the donor is open or anonymous. Kyle says that the blood type doesn't matter and neither does them being open or anonymous matter. Auntie Hattie then asks what that means. Amber begins to explain, "Anonymous means that the donor does not agree up front to possible contact with an offspring when they turn 18; whereas the open donor agrees that when an offspring turns 18 and would like some type of contact, they are willing. She explains that there is a cost difference between the two and they don't care which type is selected because they plan on telling the child from where they came when it's appropriate. Everyone continues with their search when Ben then asks, "Can we also select donors with ICI (intracervical) or IUI (intrauterine) samples. Kyle responds with a yes and explains that the IUI or ICI samples can be used for an IVF procedure. Ben gets it and proceeds with their search. All groups are quiet. Everyone is concentrating on the task at hand and all you can hear is the keys on the keyboard clicking to their own little beat. We work on this for hours. From our initial search we came up with a total of 192 donors. We then cut donors by height because the search gave us one height range from 5'10 to 6'0 so we were able to cut out the guys that were 5'10 and 5'11, which then brought our list down to 125.

Next, we eliminate donors by the free information provided such as their short profiles, staff impressions, essays, and brief medical history. After this we were left with 20 selections, Phoenix and Ben were down to 32 and Amber and Kyle were down to 11. They had already been searching so they had a head start. One good thing is that we all had 9 donors that showed up on all of our lists so Amber and Kyle made the decision that we would only focus on those 9 since we all selected them. Amber said, "This is a sign that these guys made the cut". When we finished, we are all exhausted. Phoenix didn't want anyone to leave since we had been up all night working on operation baby Monroe. So he and Auntie Hattie made sleeping arrangements for all to stay the night. We all wake up to Auntie Hattie doing what she normally does, cooking. Everyone ate, we have brief conversation and they all go their separate ways. Phoenix and I head to the hospital. We are so excited; the twins should be home this week as they have stayed on course since their early arrival. They're gaining weight, eating on their own and it's close to their delivery date. We have everything ready for them to come home. We have the room set up with the cribs, dressers, changing tables, clothes, an abundance of diapers and everything else we need. We've made arrangements for a nurse to assist with the twins for a couple of weeks to make sure we are doing what we're suppose to and they are okay and have no difficulties adjusting. Amber, CoCo and Auntie Hattie insist on giving us a shower once the twins

142

get home and we get settled. After much protest from Phoenix and I, we finally agree to something small, at the house and more of a coming home celebrating for the twins and for Justin. The twins will be home for a week when Justin is released. Amber and Kyle have offered to let Justin stay with them, well not quite with them per se. They have a cute little back house that's separate from theirs. It's a one-bedroom, one bath that will be perfect for him. Even though he's only been away for a year, Amber feels it's necessary that he gets with a program or organization that deals with and is dedicated to helping those who have been released from jail get back on their feet. Their property has been vacant for a few months and Amber suggested they save it for her brother and Kyle was totally fine with it. The last time Amber spoke with Justin, he indicated he would need anger management as a stipulation to his parole. Again, Amber is being very proactive and has set up his sessions for him. She's being the big sister and trying to make his transition home easy but Kyle is telling her Justin has to stand on his own two feet and take responsibility by making his appointments as well as other meetings. He feels that they are already giving him a head start by providing him with a place to stay. Justin doesn't have to worry about money because we got him as far as cash is concerned but again as a stipulation of his parole, he will need to find a job. Justin is ready and has learned a valuable lesson. He told us he had a lot of time to think about his mistakes and bad decisions and for one, he will never put his hands on another woman. Outside of his anger management classes, he has agreed to family counseling with Amber and me. Although he was just a child when he killed the man that molested my sister and me, he has never been the same and that incident has impacted his life and pretty much was a precursor to how his life would play out. After our parents died, Amber did the best she could raising us, as she was still a child herself. We didn't have any real, positive male role models in our life. We were all each other had. Justin will learn that he has to accept who he is but he also has the ability to change. It will take him some time but he has the support of all of us. Even though Phoenix and Ben are not that much older than he is, they will still be good role models for him. When I look at the big picture, we are all starting over and have new beginnings and I'm truly looking forward to what life has in store for all of us. We have each other and we will move through these rough times as we always do, because we are fighters, survivors. Funny how our paths cross, we all have a story, we all have baggage, and drama. It's all about how we process and deal with it. Shit, we have to learn from our mistakes and keep it pushing.

We have been getting calls from the media asking for interviews regarding the upcoming sentencing of Rocky. Detective Watson suggests that we do not do any interviews or speak to the media at all. We all know how they take one thing you say and make it into something totally different. So to make sure that doesn't happen, we have agreed that no one says anything. There have been a number of interviews since this incident happened. Initially the detectives gave a statement at the hospital, then another regarding the officer killed and the other injured in the line of duty. There was coverage at the officer's funeral; not only was he a well respected and decorative officer, he was the first undercover officer killed in the line of duty in 30 years. So needless to say, he had a grand send off. There were officers that came from near and far to support their fallen officer. It was a compelling service; we did not attend but watched with broken hearts as each channel in the Bay Area televised the service. His wife, two children, friends and family members stood next to his casket with falling tears and broken hearts, knowing that their daddy, husband and loved one was never coming home. His sons 9 and 6 years old, stood before hundreds of people and read a poem they wrote and a poem they found. Bret, the 6 year old, read their poem and Bobby read the one they found by Douglas J. Watson; they altered it a bit to fit them.

Daddy,

We will be big boys and try not to cry but we are so sad the bad guy made you go to the big place in the sky. We will miss you taking us to soccer practice, and helping us with our coats and we will miss you taking us out on the fishing boat. Me and Bobby will remember not to be loud cause even though you are in the sky we will still make you proud. We love you daddy and we hope you like it.

Fishing With Dad

We remember our dad waking us up at 4 o'clock, barely getting up with our eyes half-shut. Getting ready and packing up the truck, hoping to catch some fish down on the dock. Driving to the lake still dark, watching dad drive and listening to our dogs bark. Thinking this time I'll make my mark, and just hoping to catch the big one. On the boat driving around, knowing we won't be leaving with a frown. Cause we're with our dad and he knows best, because he's wearing his famous fishing vest. Tying the hooks on my line, to bait this pole isn't mine. Dad said he'll buy us one when we're older and maybe a little bolder. We love our daddy so much and we know he loves us too. His love for us is stronger than glue, and that's why we wrote this for you. Dad, if you are listening, we love you so; you are the reason why we'll grow.

There was not a dry eye in the church once Bobby finished reading the poem. There was not a dry eye in our house as you could hear sniffles from around the family room. I was so surprised that he didn't break but he stood tall and delivered a wonderful poem for his dad. One that I'm sure he was looking down and is very proud. Cameron's family requested that media not show, again they wanted the service to just be close friends and family and believe it or not, they respected the family's wishes. However, I did see an interview with a family member. I think it was his uncle looking for his fifteen minutes of fame. X's family allowed the media, just not inside the sanctuary. They asked a few questions to some exiting the service, but we dodged them like the plague and made a beeline straight to the car and out of there, not to get caught up. Sometimes it's hard not to react and ignore someone shoving a microphone in your face every time you leave your home, hospital, or wherever.

Chapter 21

Today is going to be a trying, emotional and long day. This is the day Rocky will receive his sentence. I know in my gut that it's not going to be good. I mean he killed 3 people and with one being a cop. They are going to fry his ass like they do some extra crispy chicken at KFC. How is it that you still have love for someone knowing that they have done wrong, done you wrong? I guess when you've known someone for a while, you just can't turn off the love. You can be mad as hell and hurt beyond measure but you just can't turn off love like it's a switch. Well at least I can't. Some people are just evil and have no heart and it's easy for them to say fuck it and fuck you. It's really sad but it is what it is. I can't worry about people and their delusions of perfect; you know the ones who do no wrong? They are so perfect that when those around them are less than perfect (in their eyes), they cut them off when really they need to see the shit and dirt they do and learn how to deal with the truth before they point their fingers and judge others for what they do. Just because you don't agree with something, doesn't make it wrong. I'm hoping that Rocky has at least done that. I hope he realizes he is not perfect and come to grips with his demons. I remember him telling me he gave me signs and hints that he loved me and wanted to be with me and I missed it. Maybe I just didn't pick up on them because he was insane and made up a bunch of shit in his mind. I'm thinking maybe he thought he did and when you tell yourself something so many times you believe it when you really didn't say or do anything at all. You just live in this make-believe, this fantasy world. Well in real life when someone shows you who they are...believe them! Rocky is fake and phony. He played a real good game. I thought he really had my back and was happy for me, when he was hating all along. Smiled in my face and thought a certain way about me, boy with friends like this, who needs enemies? I'm devastated that he hurt so many people but I'm sure all dogs will have their day. Even though he really showed his ass, I'm sure with his attitude and personality he's hurt so many others along the way, but he was so good at hiding it. All I can say is karma is a bitch and he will be punished for the crimes he committed and I'm sure he will also pay for all the hurt he's caused people. One cannot do harm to others and think that their lives will be a bed of roses. It might be today or tomorrow or even next year but my thought is that you just can't keep doing people wrong and think your life is going to be a bed of roses. Your day is coming and it might be sooner than you think, I pray he can handle it. A good friend told me that if you cut somebody off that is near and dear to your heart, chances are they gave you the scissors. Real talk. Well in this case, Rocky really gave me the scissors. I also heard that if someone shows you who they are…believe them! As mad as I am, I'm really trying to deal with this as it is still a shock and believe it or not, I care about what happens to him.

Phoenix and I are getting ready for court today. Auntie Hattie's ready and in the kitchen fussing about something. When we reach the kitchen, she wants us to eat because we don't know how long the court session is going to last and says it's important we have energy to deal with what is going to happen today. Phoenix blesses the food and we eat pancakes, sausage, bacon, potatoes and eggs in silence. Ben calls to let us know he and CoCo will meet us there and Ambers sends a text saying the same. I grab my bag and keys and Auntie Hattie and I head for the door. Phoenix is dragging behind as he left something in the room. He locks the front door and we wait for the elevator to arrive. Everyone has a melancholy mood as to be expected but we need to come out of this funk or my head is going to explode. The silence is killing me. After entering the elevator, Phoenix holds my hand and whispers he loves me in my ear. He then says, "I'm glad this is almost over." Auntie Hattie and I agree. Once in the car, he turns the radio on and Will Downing is crooning through the speakers. The music is calming but not doing so much for my sour stomach. I search my purse for a soft peppermint with the hopes that it will settle my stomach and plus I love the way they melt in my mouth. I remember my grandmother always carried a zip lock baggy with soft and hard peppermints, gum, and halls cough drops in her purse. I always drop a handful in my purse just in case. After popping it in my mouth, I offer Auntie Hattie and Phoenix one, they both accept. Driving across the Bay Bridge, we run into some traffic. It takes us a little longer to get across and we are running short on time before court starts at 8:30. I'm in no hurry to get there but I can tell Phoenix is frustrated because of the unexpected traffic and we left early to prepare for any. Oh well, shit happens and everything happens for a reason. We finally make it to the courthouse and it looks like a circus. There are hundreds of people flooding the front of the building, the street, and sidewalks. There are police out trying to keep order of the crowd. We're directed by a traffic cop to pull in front of the building. Phoenix tells us to hang on for a second before we exit the car. He pulls out his cell phone and sends a text. Within seconds his phone dings with a text message. I'm looking at him when I'm startled by a knock on the passenger side window. After jumping out of my pumps because it scared the shit out of me, I tell you I'm so damn jumpy now, anyway, I turn to see Detective Watson standing outside the door. Phoenix told Auntie Hattie and I that the detective will walk us up and he's going to park the car and will meet us in there. Auntie Hattie and I exit the car. The detective and an officer press us through the crowd. There are so many people, it's scary. I hate crowds, especially crowds of this magnitude in such close proximity. There are so many people screaming at us. The media is shouting out questions and they're coming from every direction. We make it in unharmed. There seems to be just as many people inside as there is out. We get to go through the fast lane so to speak, meaning we don't have to wait in the security line. Once through the line, we wait for on Phoenix for a few minutes. It is past 8:30a.m. but we don't care. We're dealing with black folks; they're never on time. Phoenix finally makes it through the front door and the detective gets him to the fast lane. Once we are all together, we make our way to the courtroom. The media is having a field day with this. This is probably the biggest court case since that famous football player was charged for allegedly killing his estranged wife and boyfriend or friend, in Southern California some years back. We make it to the courtroom but before we enter, Auntie Hattie and I run to the ladies room across the hall to release our bladders before we enter the courtroom. As soon as we walk into the courtroom, all eyes are on us. My anxiety heightens and I feel like I can't breathe. Phoenix senses my discomfort and whispers to me to try and relax. He squeezes my hand, letting me know all is going to be okay. I look at him and smile trying my best to believe him. The courtroom is filled to capacity. There's standing room only. People line the wall packed in like sardines. I scan the room and of course I see Keisha and her crazy ass family. If looks could kill, I would drop to the ground right where I stand. I then spot Amber, Kyle, Ben and CoCo. Ben waves his hand, motioning us in his direction as he has saved us seats. We take our seats and quietly say hello to everyone on our row, which includes the usual. There's small chatter throughout the courtroom and the lawyers sit at the tables on either side of the room. They're shuffling papers around and whispering to their co-lawyers or assistants. The bailiff commands everyone to stand as the judge enters the courtroom. Once the judge enters and the bailiff announces who he is, he tells us to be seated. He retrieves some documents and begins to read to himself. The judge tells the courtroom that he is only going to allow two T.V. stations in the courtroom. There were some sounds of disappointment. The judge tells the media that channels 4 and 7 may stay and the rest had to leave. The stations that had to leave were upset but left without a fight because the judge has a history of throwing people in jail who challenge him. Once they left, it also freed up some room because there was barely room to stand. Time is ticking away. We all sit in silence waiting for Rocky to appear. I look at my watch and I know we were already late and now it's past 9:00a.m. and it seems they are still running behind. The lawyers check the time too as the judge asks, "Do we have a problem counsel?" The lawyers are looking at each other like they are crazy. They're expecting one or the other to respond to the judge because they have no idea why Rocky is not there yet. He was supposed to be transported and in the courtroom at 8:30 and it's now 9:30 and still no Rocky. Finally the public defender says, "Your honor, we were expecting him by 8:30. I'm not sure what the holdup is but I'm sure they are stuck in traffic because we have not received any calls stating otherwise." The judge obviously annoyed says, "We will wait 30 minutes, until 10:00 for them to get here then we will need to reschedule. I will not have my entire day pushed back because this case is running late." He then asks if they understand and they respond with a yes. The public defender sends her assistant out the courtroom to see if she can find out what the delay is. Detective Watson's cell phone vibrates. He pulls his cell phone out of the inside pocket of his black suit jacket and looks at the caller ID. He answers, telling the caller to hang on a second. He excuses himself and exits the courtroom.

Chapter 22

Rocky is getting ready for his big day in court. He pretty much knows the outcome will not be good but will deal with whatever. Rocky is somewhat scared but he will never show it. He has always been a tough guy and this situation will not make him be any other way. It will not break him down or make him weak. He'll have to stay strong no matter what. He sits in his cell reflecting on all that has transpired. He is sorry that he got caught up in this so-called love triangle. But he's not sorry that he finally stood up for what he believed in, and what he believed in was the love he has for Sydney. He's sorry that the cop got in the way and feels bad that he left behind a wife and kids. He felt a little emotional watching his funeral service but then thought, sometimes there's causalities of war and he knew the job was dangerous when he took it....shit happens. He thought how it brought him happiness when he found out Cameron was dead but his bubble was busted when he found out Phoenix and his sidekick Ben was still alive. He was sure thinking that the bullet with Phoenix's name on it would be a fatal one. As he sits and thinks he probably should have went with Plan B, but he got caught up. If he had went for Plan B, he wouldn't have been so close to all that went down. Well, he thinks he will keep it under wraps because his targets are still alive and kicking. And there's nothing he can do about it now, what's done is done. What he really wants is for Sydney to understand what he did was for her and if she can get that through her thick skull, she will be able to forgive him and they can move on. "I protected her. I always had her back and the list goes on for the things I did for her, but that selfish bitch didn't see anything I did or said. And they say I'm crazy? Nah, that bitch is crazy and couldn't see the forest for the trees," Rocky says out loud. As the thoughts and words come out of his mouth, he thinks how he can love her and hate her all in the same breath. Her loss, he thinks. She'll see how much I love her when I'm gone...locked up for God knows how long. She'll come around and I'll be right here waiting for her with open arms. Rocky thinks that, that rich motherfucker can keep her occupied until daddy comes home. He doesn't know why she's with him anyway because he ain't even her type. "I mean, I get dude is loaded but hell he's shorter than she likes them and he's one of them yellow dudes who thinks light skin is coming back," he laughs to himself. I don't know what he has that I don't, well other than money, he thinks.

Rocky decides not to wear the suit Keisha brought him for court today. He thought it would not make a difference how he looks because he would just have to come right back here and to his orange monkey suit. Before he was brought back to his cell this morning after having breakfast with the other level 3 and 4 inmates, he ran into a little situation. The inmates were being ushered in and he made eye contact with Justin who was going out. This has happened before and he is glad that he has not had a face to face with him just yet. He knows it's coming and bound to happen, he doesn't know when but he will be ready for anything when it does. Rocky is told to eat his breakfast faster than usual because a guard told him they need to leave for the courthouse in an hour. Rocky did as he was told and tries to finish the disgusting food in record time. Rocky looks up and sees some of the other inmates

154

staring at him and it's confirmed he really has to watch his back. He finishes his food and stands to leave and one of the guards in the back of the chow hall motions for him to make his way to the back. While leaving the chow hall and heading back to his cell, the guard tells him he needs to shower, get dressed and they will be leaving soon. He makes it back to his cell and grabs his stuff to shower and get dressed. Rocky takes his shower quick and is ready to go back to his cell to get dressed. As they walk down the corridor, Rocky feels something like a sting hit him on the side of his face. He rubs his face and there's something sticking out of his skin. He tries to pull it out but cannot grip it. He yelps, "Fuck!" The guard asks what's wrong and sees him holding the right side of his face. When Rocky moves his hand from his cheek, the guard notices that his face is swelling and knows immediately what just happened. "I don't know but it hurts like hell and my face is swelling and feels numb. There is still something stuck in my face," he says. Still walking, the guard says nothing but whispers to another passing guard and they both burst out in laughter. Rocky asks them what the hell was so damn funny. "Oh man, you got the shit dart. You better take him to the infirmary fast before the pain really kicks in," he says to the other guard. The guard walking with Rocky tells him they will need to stop at the infirmary because the doc will need to take a look at his face so they head in that direction. Before reaching the infirmary, Rocky notices that two inmates are heading in his direction. His heart starts to pound fast. He senses that something is about to go down. The inmates approach him and the guard and both start to laugh. One inmate says, "Damn homie, you look like a

155

chipmunk and your face is fucked up man." Rocky still holding his face asks, "What the hell happened to me?" The other inmate laughing uncontrollably says, "You got popped with a shit dart." "What the hell is that?" Rocky inquires. "Okay newbie, let me break it down for you. Some inmates find staples from papers or magazines. They straighten them out then soak it in their own shit. Once the shit dart soaks for a few days, they take some paper or a straw, roll it up and place the shit soaked dart at the base of the paper or straw and when they see a target, in this case you, they blow into it and it comes flying right into a part of the body, mainly an exposed body part, like the face, neck, arms, etc. Just like you used to blow spit balls when you were a kid, same concept but these my brother are lethal. So I'm thinking you must have done some fucked up shit because they got the best to shoot you, and they only get one chance and they got you. You'll be okay man, nothing a little drugs from the doc can't fix," he explains while he and his friend walk away still laughing.

The thought of someone spitting a dart soaked in shit made Rocky sick to his stomach. He didn't think the shit was funny at all but thought it could have been worse. He's glad it wasn't worse, well at least not today. He thinks that they are really messing with him now. First it was his nose, now it's shit darts. Either way he didn't think the shit was funny at all. He felt that either he was getting this treatment because he's the new kid on the block per say or someone (Justin) is out to get him. He truly believes it's the latter because from the moment he's been here he's been in protective custody. Even though everyone is laughing at his expense, they continue on to the infirmary. Once they reach

156

the infirmary, the doctor is on the phone and waves them in acknowledging their presence. The doctor finishes his call and asks how he can help him. When he realizes it was Rocky he says laughing, "You back so soon, what is it now? Never mind I can see why you're here, looks like you got in the way of a feces dart." "I don't know why everyone finds this so fucking amusing. This shit hurts like hell! Are you going to give me something to kill the pain doc or are you going to keep fucking laughing or do your damn job!" Rocky shouts with an attitude. The doctor tells the guard to go to the next office to get some bandages and alcohol swabs. The guard walks out of the room they are in and in to the next to get what the doctor requested. The doctor tells Rocky to sit in the chair next to the hospital bed. He opens a drawer and tells Rocky to roll up his sleeve and he does as he's told. The doctor then puts a tourniquet around Rocky's arm and slaps his arm to get a good vein. Rocky finds it odd that he's getting a shot in the veins instead of his upper arm or butt but he doesn't question it because he figures the good doc knows what he's doing.

Chapter 23

The doctor has two syringes on the counter. He injects one then the other. He removes the tourniquet and tells Rocky to undress so that he can give him a shot in his butt. Rocky says, "Damn, 3 shots? This must be some powerful shit, literally." The doctor does not respond and the guard comes back letting the doctor know he could not find the items he sent him for. He tells him it's okay and that someone must have removed them. Rocky is ready to get back to his cell so he can quickly change so they can leave for the courthouse. While walking back to his cell, the same two inmates who passed him going to the infirmary were now coming towards him again. "Hope you feeling better my man," one of them says. Rocky thinks that he doesn't feel as much pain as he had before. By the time they reach his cell, he tells the guard he doesn't feel well. The guard tells him it's just the effects of the shit dart and the meds the doc gave him. He tells him to go ahead and get ready so they can leave because they are already running late. Another guard came and he and the original guard are outside of Rocky's cell having a conversation. Rocky sits on his cot because he feels light headed and feels like his heart is racing and about to pop out of his chest. He starts to sweat profusely and is finding it hard to breathe. Rocky tries to call out for the guards but couldn't get the words out. Within seconds, Rocky collapses on the floor of his cell. He's trying desperately to catch his breath but is having difficulty. His eyes are open and he wants to speak but again nothing comes out and it was like his body was frozen. Finally one of the guards was wondering what the hell is taking him so long to get ready. The guard now walks a couple feet to Rocky's cell to find him on the floor. He calls out to the other guard then on his radio to ask for help. Three additional guards came to assist with Rocky. They get Rocky on the stretcher and rush him to the infirmary, yet again. This time the doctor knew he was coming and calls for some of the additional doctors on staff for assistance. On the way to the infirmary, Rocky's body starts to convulse; he's foaming at the mouth, and his eyes have just rolled in the back of his head. One of the guards screams, "We're losing him, it looks like he stopped breathing. Hurry up dammit! We gotta get him there now!" They get Rocky to the infirmary and four doctors are waiting for his arrival. They take over the stretcher and rush him in the room. One doctor is barking out orders and the others are following his orders. They are behind the curtain and the guards cannot see what is going on. They can however hear a doctor saying, "Clear!" The guards assume his heart stopped and they are using the defibrillator trying to restart it. One of the doctors comes from behind the curtain and closes the main door blocking the guards from hearing anything now. A few minutes later, the warden and investigation unit arrive at the infirmary. The warden lets the guards know that there will be a full investigation and he will need to let the investigation unit also known as the 'Goon Squad' handle it from here. The investigation unit is in place so that when an inmate gets seriously hurt or killed, they are the ones who find out what happened, and who was involved. The commander of the goon squad takes the guards to an office so they can get started with the investigation while the information is still fresh in the guards' minds. They get started with the guard that was with Rocky from the time he came and got him hours ago for breakfast. He gives each account in great detail from when the other inmates passes them in the hall twice, to no one going in or out of his cell. He explains that Rocky told him he was not feeling well and that he told him it was because of the shit dart and probably the meds and that he needed to hurry and get dressed because they were running late transporting him to the courthouse.

The commander is writing everything down; asking the guard did he think it was strange that the same inmates passed them twice. The guard indicates that he didn't deem it strange due to them passing inmates a number of times a day, which is not out of the normal. He says that the inmates were not causing trouble; they stopped us and talked about how Rocky's face was swollen from getting hit with a shit dart. The guard continues on about what happened after they left the infirmary from him getting a shot to him taking his shower. The guard explains, they were with him at all times and also right outside his cell and he brought him back to get dressed for court. The commander asks a few more questions then they all leave to get back to the infirmary. The warden is there speaking with the doctors as the investigation unit and the guards approach. The look on their faces is not good. The doctor explains that from the symptoms they saw when he was brought in, the foaming at the mouth, the sweating and convulsing, it appears he suffered from a drug overdose. The warden then explains that they are having a serious drug problem and have been trying to put an end to it or at least slow down the trafficking until they can put a stop to it. This has been a problem for years, it didn't happen overnight, therefore, it can't be fixed overnight, however, they are doing their best with the resources they have. He also explains that Rocky makes the 5th inmate to have an apparent drug overdose in the past three months. And, they don't think it's foul play or attempted suicide. These guys are in here for some serious crimes and maybe they just get fed up with life and this is the way to try and end it. "Does it make it right? Of course not, but like I said we are doing our best to bring an end to the drug trafficking," the warden explains. The doctor indicates that the other inmates came in the same way and their symptoms were the same, except for one. He actually came in with the syringe still in his arm and once the test results were done the results showed that they had a large amount of drugs in their systems. The doctor did say that he could not be certain but that would be his best guess. The warden tells the investigation unit that he wants a full search and a report on his desk within the next couple of hours. The word spread fast through the unit that the goon squad was on the way. In the level that Rocky was on, the guards ran a pretty tight shift because most of the inmates were being kept there because of threats and they wanted to keep them safe until they were transferred to their final residence. One would think that it's hard to sneak things in the prison but people get really creative. Yes, visitors are searched when entering and before they can see the inmate but sometimes, stuff slips through. They do cavity searches when the inmates come through but with visitors that might not happen. It will depend on what inmate is being visited. If the inmate is known for certain crimes then their visitors might have to have what they call a 'Keister' search, which means someone could be hiding drugs or God knows what up their asses. It really makes no since that someone would risk their life to smuggle drugs in jail and take another risk of getting caught. But people are just stupid like that. Right after the guards rushed Rocky to the infirmary, the guards ordered a lock down of the unit, which means all inmates had to return to their cells and they are locked in. The goon squad interviewed each inmate on the unit to see if anyone saw or heard anything. Of course no one heard or saw anything. The inmate code is something of that like the police department, they protect their own, and therefore, everyone turns on a blind eye and deaf ear. Even if the inmates don't get along, they will not say anything, one because if they have an issue with the inmate in question, they will handle it on their own and two because no one wants to be labeled a snitch. Rocky's cell was midway through the unit. The goon squad started at both ends of the unit. The commander wanted to save Rocky's cell for last. Their search didn't find anything out of the normal and no one was taken into custody. When all this went down, the unit had already had breakfast and were out on the yard for their 6-hour exercise day. So, no one should have been in their cells during this time. But as we know, when a plan is put into place, there's no limit to the resources they have to get the job at hand...done. With no leads and no evidence from any of the other inmates or their cells, the investigative team is at a dead end. The commander says, "Let's move into Rocky's cell and begin the search. Hopefully we will find something that gives us some leads as to what happened. I'm hoping he just had some type of reaction to the shit dart and the meds the doctor gave him. We haven't seen anything like it before but every person is different and maybe an allergic reaction caused his death." The goon squad conducts the search of Rocky's cell and are shocked at what they find.

Chapter 24

Detective Watson enters the courtroom and stands in the back trying to gather his thoughts. He waits for a second before he starts back to his seat but before he does the courtroom phone rings at the bailiff's desk and stops him in his tracks. It's interesting because the entire courtroom gets quiet; I guess finding it odd that the courtroom phone is ringing. The bailiff answers the phone. He says nothing, just listens. Once the call is done, he hangs up the receiver and walks over to the judge, whispering in his ear. The bailiff then returns to his rightful seat in the courtroom and begins to gather his papers that are on the desk. The judge clears his throat and says, "We need a 15-minute recess and I need counsel in my chambers right now." Chatter erupts throughout the courtroom; everyone is wondering what the hell is going on. The judge stands and exits the courtroom with the prosecutor and public defender on his heels. I look around the courtroom wondering where the detective was. My eyes reach the back of the room and there he stands with a disturbed look on his face. He makes eye contact with me and starts walking in the direction of our seats. He takes the same seat he had before he got a call and holds his head down. I have a bad feeling in the pit of my stomach. Something is not right. The people in the courtroom are getting louder with their group and individual conversations. It feels like a weird energy has filled the room. I look at Phoenix and say to him, "Babe, I wonder what's going on. I have a real bad feeling something is wrong." Phoenix tells me not to worry and that he's sure everything is okay. He says that delays happen all the time and they will get started after the brief recess. I'm praying he's right but again this feeling in my gut is telling me otherwise. I ask Phoenix to switch seats with me so I can sit next to Detective Watson. I look at the detective and the look in his eyes confirms something is wrong, something is seriously wrong. "Detective Watson, do you know what's going on? Why are we running so late? Where is Rocky? Did something happen?" All these questions are spilling out my mouth and before the detective can answer, I'm asking another. The detective sits there in silence, staring into space, completely ignoring my questions and me. I tap him on the leg to bring him out of the daydreaming state and ask my questions again. The detective begins to speak but the bailiff tells the courtroom to rise as the judge is re-entering the courtroom. The counsel follows behind him and head to their respective places. It's hard to get a read as to what is happening because everyone has on their poker faces. The courtroom stands, the judge enters, takes his seat and we all sit back down. The courtroom is quiet and it appears all are holding their breath waiting to hear what he has to say. The public defender whispers in his assistant's ear. They both gather papers and documents off the table in front of them, push their seats back, and proceed to exit at the back of the courtroom. Keisha screams, "Where da hell y'all goin!? You need to be here to help my brotha get off or get a good sentence. He don't know da right thangs to ax." Neither one of them says a word; they keep walking and exit the courtroom. Within seconds we all notice the prosecutor is now doing the same thing, packing up. She and her co-prosecutor also leave the courtroom. Everyone starts to ask questions and the courtroom participants are clearly confused. The back doors open and six sheriffs enter, blocking the doors. Looks of concern now fill the room.

The judge hits his gavel to gain order in the court. Apparently no one hears it as everyone is still talking amongst themselves. He hits it a few more times and then yells, "Order in the court!" over the microphone placed in front of him. This time he got everyone's attention. Those who were talking were now quiet and those that were standing are now sitting, and everyone looks in the direction of the judge. The judge clears his throat and hesitates before he speaks. "This is quite difficult," he pauses. Keisha screams again, "Why did they leave!? What is happin? Where is my brotha? Yo honer." The courtroom erupts with a bunch of, "Yeah we need some answers. We need to know what is going on and we need to know now!" someone shouts. The judge hits his gavel again and tells the courtroom to settle down. "As I was saying, this is difficult. But we have cancelled the sentencing hearing and all charges have been dropped." Before he could finish, Rocky's friends and family with Keisha as their ringleader burst out once again, this time celebrating as they think they have won, whereas the friends and family members of the victims are in complete and utter shock. I feel myself getting ready to stand and protest with the victims' family members when the detective places his hand on my leg and tells me to relax and let the judge finish what he has to say. I look at him like he is crazy, one for touching my leg and two for telling me to relax. Did this fool just hear what the judge said? They're dropping all the charges and letting that crazy ass fool killer go? I still love Rocky, but regardless as to how I feel about him, he still needs to pay for his crimes. How do they let a cop killer and a person with a long laundry list of other crimes and charges off? "Just like that, the case is closed? What the fuck?" I ask myself. Phoenix must have sensed I was about to lose it and grabs my hand. "Baby, I know you are upset, we all are but I need you not to blow up and wind up in jail." I look at him with tears in my eyes and a feeling of defeat. I glance at the friends and family and they display the same look. This has to be a nightmare because shit like this doesn't happen in real life. The judge hits his gavel once again and screams into the microphone to get order in his courtroom. People start to settle down and the judge then tells them he was not finished with what he had to say before he was rudely interrupted by certain participants who started celebrating a bit prematurely. He continues, "Now I'm going to continue with what I need to say. I do not want one damn interruption. Let it be known that if there is one outburst, you will be removed from my courtroom and possibly held in contempt of court. So if none of you want to end up in jail, then I suggest you all keep quiet. Now, as I was saying, the case has been dropped due to a situation at the county jail. This morning, Rockland Foster had an apparent drug overdose. I was told he was found on the floor of his cell unresponsive. He was rushed to the infirmary immediately. The investigative unit completed a search of the unit and interviewed all inmates associated and housed in and with that unit. Their search came up empty, not finding anything or no one seeing anything. However, when Mr. Foster's cell was searched, the investigators found 4 syringes with a tourniquet under his mattress. With the materials found in his cell, the warden ruled out foul play and deemed this situation as self-affliction. The medical staff did everything they could but unfortunately, Mr. Foster did not survive as a result of the overdose." The courtroom is again in a state of shock. I think it takes a few seconds before Keisha processes what the judge just said. "What da hell you mean he didn't survive? My brotha don't do no drugs, he ain't never did no drugs. I mean he might have smoked a little weed but that shit ain't gone kill him! Somebody dun set him up and had him killed. Yo honer you gotta find out who did dis to my brotha!" Keisha shouts. She is no longer shouting, she is now bawling out of control. Then all of a sudden, she stops crying and this evil look comes across her face, scary enough it was the same look Rocky had in the club. "I know you had somethem to do wit dis, you bitch! You had my brotha killed! He told me yo brotha was comin fo him. You will pay fo dis you bitch! You betta watch yo back cause every time you turn around, I could be dare. As a matta of fac, yo whole family betta watch out cause they can get got too. Especially dem two little babby's y'all got," she so passionately explains. I stand up because this bitch has taken this shit too far now. When you threaten my babies, we have a fucking problem. The detective gets on his phone and is sending a text to someone. Phoenix pulls me down and tells me not to say a word. I'm burning up and I want to leap across these chairs and strangle this illiterate ghetto-ass bitch. "That's right, calm yo hoe down fo she get dis ass whippem imma give her," Keisha spits. The judge hits his gavel and tells Keisha that he has had enough of her. He says he knows she's upset with the recent news of her brother but he has warned her many times about threatening people in his courtroom and reminds her that if any harm comes to anyone involved in this case that he personally will make sure she spends the rest of her life in prison. He then tells the officers at the back of the courtroom to remove her before he throws her in jail now. The officers appear at the end of the row where she is seated and tell her to come with them. She makes her way past the people who are sitting next to her while shouting some obscenities, "Fuck all y'all! Somebody gonna pay for my brotha dying! I don't give a shit what da judge say, you betta watch yo back. Cause best believe I'm coming fo you!" With that, she was removed from the courtroom and her family and friends follow.

Chapter 25

We are all frozen and in a state of shock. The media is having a field day with this. As soon as the news was delivered, they scattered like roaches when the lights come on. The judge tells the people who remain in his courtroom that he has never experienced such a circus of people before. He explains he has seen some things throughout his career but this case by far takes the cake. He tells me that if I feel threatened by that lady, the detective will make sure she does me no harm. He tells me to make sure I contact the police as he is going to issue me and all parties involved restraining orders. Detective Watson tells us that he put officers on duty at the hospital until the babies come home and we are truly grateful for that as well as everything else he has done. He says, "Wow. I was not expecting that. I got the call right before they called the courtroom and I was and still am in a state of shock. I have no words." Auntie Hattie says, "No one does, I'm sure. This is way too much to process for one day. Let's get out of here." Detective Watson tells us that it would be best if we can exit out the back of the building to avoid the reporters. Auntie Hattie lets everyone know that if they want to come over for some food, she's sure Phoenix wouldn't mind. Everyone looks at Phoenix for the approval and he says, "I don't mind but Sydney and I are on the way to the hospital to check on the twins. We all gather our belongings and follow the detective to the back of the courthouse to possibly avoid the media. Once we make our way to the back, there are four Escalades parked in back. The detective tells us he thought we might need these. Ben says, "We'll come back for our cars later, but right now let's get the hell out of here." We all hop in the trucks and tell the drivers where we want to go. Phoenix and I head to the hospital. On the ride over, we talk about how unbelievable all of this is. "I cannot believe that Rocky is dead and from a drug overdose no less. I've known Rocky for years and one thing I will agree with his crazy ass sister, is that he didn't do drugs. There are so many things running through my mind that I can't keep up. Did he start in jail? Was this really a suicide or did someone really kill him?" Phoenix tells me to try not to think about it because it will kill me trying to figure it out. I say a prayer asking God to please not let Justin be involved. He only has a week left and I need him to be home with his family. Phoenix asks if I'm okay and I tell him no. I tell him I'm so upset at what Rocky did but I never wanted him dead. I didn't want anyone dead or hurt for that matter. "Enough is enough!" I scream. Phoenix tells me he knows how I feel and really wishes that things turned out better than they did. We ride the rest of the way in silence and in each other's arms. When we reach the hospital, there are two officers just as the detective mentioned. The twin's doctor is there and we get the latest updates on their progress. We were shocked and overly excited all at the same time. The doctor tells us we can take our babies home today. Phoenix and I are in tears, as we cannot believe we finally get to bring our son, River Zaire and daughter, China Reign home. I look at Phoenix and tell him that we will need to leave to get their car seats and bags with clothes to prepare them for the trip home. He tells me not to worry. He had Auntie Hattie pack their bags and he brought them and their car seats up here a few weeks ago. He reminds me that his aunt always says, "If you stay ready, you don't have to get ready." We both laugh. I check with the NICU nurse and confirm that we can take the babies home. Phoenix contacts the in-home nurse we hired to let her know we are bringing the babies home sooner than expected.

We choose not to call Auntie Hattie to tell her what is happening so that when we arrive home, she will be surprised. Hopefully everyone will be there for dinner so they will be surprised too. We had the driver that brought us to the hospital stay there until he took us home. We explained to him that our car was back at the courthouse and we would pay whatever the cost to have him hang out to wait for us. The driver said he would call his office to make sure he could be available. He told us that he would be on what they call 'AD' (as directed) which means he will be at our disposal all day until we release him. He was originally hired by the detective so we had to release him from the detective's credit card and placed under ours. Phoenix takes the car seats down to the Escalade and he and the driver are trying to put them in correctly when some SF paramedics were leaving the hospital and saw the two men struggling. They offer some assistance and were able to hook up the seats in record time. Phoenix thanks the paramedics and makes his way back up to the NICU to get ready to bring his babies home. When he returns to the NICU, he witnesses the most beautiful thing he had ever seen, his soon-to-be wife breast-feeding their son for the first time. I look up and see Phoenix staring at me with tears in his eyes. He's so emotional, and I love that he's not afraid to show it. To me, it makes him more of a man. He enters the room and kisses me on the forehead. He says to me, "Baby I love you so much and I love our children. You have made me a very happy man." "I love you too honey, now stop being a crybaby and help the nurse get Reign dressed so we can leave." After I feed the twins for the first time, the doctor and nurse want to make sure they don't have any issues with breathing or throwing up after they've been fed. River weighs a whopping 5 lbs; 4 oz and Reign came in at 4 lbs, 9 oz. Both are 19 inches long. I'm so happy that they are fine. I would have lost my mind if anything would've happened to them. We say our emotional goodbyes and head for the car. While waiting for the elevator, this woman comes up and waits with us. As we enter the elevator she's smiling and admiring how adorable the twins are. She gets off the elevator on the floor below. When the doors open she exits, turns around and her smile disappears. She says, "Keep them close to you because you never know when harm will come to them." The elevator doors close and Phoenix and I look at each other in disbelief. I ask him, "Did she just threaten our babies?" Phoenix says, "Let's hurry up and get out of here before I hurt someone." I try to put that out of my mind and think that she didn't mean what she said. She was probably trying to say something else, what I don't know, but she said 'keep them close because harm can come to them.' That's it; I'm never leaving the house. We ride home in silence until Phoenix tells me maybe we are being a little paranoid. I tell him I'm not sure but I don't want to take any chances. He then says that he will hire some bodyguards to accompany us wherever we go and I am not to leave the house without him and the bodyguards. My head hurts so I don't argue with him; I simply say, "Okay." We make it home and on the elevator with the babies safe. Phoenix tips the driver a hundred dollars and thanks him for his service. The driver tells Phoenix that if we ever need him again to give him a call, then hands him his card. Phoenix rings the doorbell and Auntie Hattie answers it, wiping her hands on her apron. She wants to scream but doesn't for fear of scaring the babies and everyone else around us. She just covers her mouth and begins to cry. Phoenix tells her not to cry and move so we can come in the house. Ben asks who is at the door and Phoenix responds "me." We walk in and to the family room where everyone is sitting. Phoenix announces that the Davenport family is finally home. Everyone turns around and the floodgates open. I think Amber is crying the most. Auntie Hattie takes River from me, still in his car seat and I go over to hug my sister. "Don't cry sis. Everything will work out and within a year you will be bringing a baby or babies home. You know those fertility drugs increase your chances for multiples. I can't wait to be an auntie as well." She tells me she knows and that her tears are that of pure joy for me and Phoenix and she couldn't be happier than to be the proud auntie of River and Reign. That's why I love my sister because she loves me for me. She doesn't judge me, think she's better than me, tries to outdo me; it's never a competition. She's as genuine as they come. When I share anything that's happening in my life, she completely supports me and again is genuinely happy for me and will do anything and everything to support my endeavors. She knows I will do the same for her. I never feel like she doesn't care nor do I feel like she has to outshine me. We are in different spaces in our lives, have different goals and admirations, but whatever they are, we support and respect each other regardless. It's never a competition. I'm her biggest cheerleader and I let her know it as much as possible. She's a strong woman and has accomplished a lot. She does not need any validations with anything she does but as I said, I'm her biggest cheerleader; therefore, I congratulate and encourage her every opportunity I get to let her know how proud of her I am, even if nobody else does. My sister is my hero and if I had a fraction of her tenacity, I would be a better person. I mean this woman was basically a single parent, raising her siblings after our parents died. She gave up her dreams to make sure we had what we needed. She sacrificed her life to take care of Justin and I when she could have walked away, but she didn't. We moved around a lot so social services wouldn't catch up with us because she was a minor. She was smart and did what my father taught her to do. Like I said, she sacrificed a lot for us and I am forever indebted to her and her struggles. Anyway, I give Amber some more encouraging words. I'm so glad we don't have that type of relationship that puts each other down, judges, and is never happy about what the other is accomplishing. The best part of our relationship is that we are open, honest, and most importantly…non judgmental. I pray that God blesses her and Kyle with a baby of their own for the simple fact that she gave up so much, and if anyone deserves it, she does. Amber hugs me, kisses me on the cheek and tells me she loves me more than words can describe. I say the same and tell her to dry her eyes, have faith and watch God work.

Chapter 26

What a week we have had. Unfortunately, Rocky died of an apparent drug overdose, the twins came home and Justin is coming home today. I turn on the T.V. to a special interview with Keisha regarding Rocky's case and death. Because his case was so publicized, the news of his death took the media and the public by surprise. Keisha is all over the news talking about how we are the cause of her brother's death. She tells the news reporter that Justin Marshall is the one who killed her brother for his sister Sydney. The reporter responds to her accusations regarding Justin and informs her that the investigation proved that Justin Marshall was nowhere near Rocky and a guard had been with him all morning so it's not fair for her to wrongfully accuse him of something he didn't do. Wow, she is really milking this situation to death; taking full advantage of her brother's death and her 15 minutes of fame. She should be mourning his death, instead of capitalizing on it or at least trying to. She has no idea that these people are making a mockery out of her. The sad part is that she keeps avoiding answering the questions as to the reason he was in jail in the first place. "He was a good person and took care of his family. He would neva hurt a fly," she says. "Yet, he killed three people, one being a cop and injured many more and you say he's a good person and would never hurt anyone. The public and the media saw the whole situation play out on T.V. so we find it very hard to believe what you say when we saw what we saw," the reporter explains. Keisha gets highly upset and is about to bring all of her ghetto out on national T.V., which is just what the public wants to see, but surprisingly she takes a deep breath and says, "Y'all don't know my brotha. I'm sure that girl pushed him to his breaking point and maybe he jus lost it." The reporter says sarcastically, "You think? And you're absolutely right, we didn't (and she emphasizes the word 'didn't') know your brother but again, the world didn't have to know him to know that only a monster could do what he did." All you saw was Keisha ball her fist and draw back; the screen fades to black then a commercial. "Oh dear Lord, this crazy woman just punched the reporter. Violence runs in the family and she allowed them to prove it on national television," I say. Wow, the buffoonery continues. I turn the T.V. off and hit the remote to the surround sound playing light jazz throughout the house. It's nice to have the house to ourselves for a change. We love our family but it's been like grand central station around here for the last 3 to 4 months. Auntie Hattie is giving the in-home nurse the blues. She will not let the poor girl do her job. Auntie Hattie is telling her what to do and what not to do. Phoenix was able to get the twins to sleep, which allowed me to sleep a little longer this morning. When I woke to an empty bed, I got nervous and ran into the twin's room. I walk into him rocking both of them in the rocking chair to sleep and softly singing them a song, I think in German. It sounds beautiful and again I think about how much more I love him. I quietly close the door and head to the family room to catch the morning news.

I must have drifted off to sleep with the jazz in the background as it is so calming and relaxing. I wake up to Phoenix on his knees kneeling in front of me. I smile at the sight of him. "Hey sleepyhead. I sent Auntie Hattie and Jackie (the nurse) home, as we are quite capable of taking care of our babies. Plus we need some alone time." I look up when I hear a noise. I look at the table next to the sofa and the baby monitor is there and is flashing. Phoenix tells me to hold on as we both listen for more movement, there was none. Phoenix says, "Now where were we? I was saying that we need some alone time and I'm not sure how much time we have so I don't want to waste it talking." I look at him with love in my eyes and wetness between my thighs. Yes, it's been a while since we have made love. We're able to sneak a little lovemaking in when we can but as new parents and still recovering from injuries, we get it in when we can. Damn, this will not always be the case. Phoenix and I both have healthy sexual appetites, so believe me, we'll make it happen. I mean we have a few opportunities for a little hanky panky but no real physical contact and heaven knows we both really need it. I sit back and say, "Well stop talking and put your lips and tongue to better use." I raise the t-shirt I'm wearing and open my legs, exposing my centerpiece, giving him a front row seat and full access. Phoenix raises an eyebrow, smiles at me, places his hands on either knee, spreading my legs wider, then dives in...head first. It's been a while so I need this moment to last for as long as it can. Somehow I am losing this battle; I can't hold it any longer and explode. Phoenix comes up for air and I tell him to switch places with me, he does. Before he sits down, I remove his sweats and almost put my eye out because as soon as I free his 'member' it's at full attention and damn near pokes me in the eyes. We both laugh and I push him down on the sofa. I spread his legs just as he did mine. I wrap my hand around his shaft and gently stroke him. He moans and relaxes some. I then take him in my mouth giving him the same amount of pleasure as I got from him. I not only like to return the gesture, I love pleasing and pleasuring my man and I do so until he explodes. He tells me to mount him and I did. I damn near go crazy because as I said, it's been a long time and I felt like a virgin again, okay maybe not quite a virgin but the centerpiece needed to be pried open. We had a good flow going and I could tell we were in sync and about to take each other to orgasmic bliss when on the down stroke one of the babies starts to cry. Phoenix tells me not to stop and to bounce harder; I did as I was told and he announces he's coming and so was I. Damn, a double explosion. This is when we are supposed to cuddle and bask in the moment. Phoenix tosses me off of him, tells me he's sorry, pulls his sweats up and says, "Daddy duty calls." He laughs and leaves me there with my ass in the air. All I could do is laugh. I get myself together and assist my soon-to-be husband with our babies.

We are getting ready for the big party tonight. Auntie Hattie, CoCo, and Amber are preparing for the coming home/baby shower celebration for the twins and Justin. We have a lot to be grateful for and I lost the battle as far as having the party. I was told to stay out and that everything is being taken care of. Kyle is picking up Justin and taking him to his new place so he can get ready for the party. I can't wait to see my baby brother. I was told Detectives Watson and Kendrick will be in attendance as well as Dr. Coverton. "Why is he coming?" I ask myself. Again against my protest, Phoenix still wants him there. He says that he owes him a great deal for saving his life and for the other stops he pulled out and he just thinks he's a cool dude regardless that he is an ex-boyfriend. I also hear that Ben's parents will be here. I'm super excited for this as well because he and Auntie Hattie are getting to know each other as mother and son but from the moment she told him who she was, he never was upset with her and completely understood her reasoning for why she did what she did. And from the beginning, he told her that he loves her and always will but his parents mean the world to him. They were the ones who raised him and he could never discount that. He feels extra special because he has two moms and when he explains that, he ends with, "Yes, I have two moms and no they are not lesbians. Not that I wouldn't mind if they were, and there is totally nothing wrong with it. In fact, I think it's sexy, my situation is just a little different." People are like, 'who gives a shit and no one cares if you were raised by a pack of wolves.' He and CoCo are getting along and I finally had a conversation with her to find out what the deal is with these two. She tells me that they are really feeling each other and confessed that he was coming to the club for months watching her dance and was scared to approach her. He also said that when he saw me he instantly had to take Phoenix there because he knew he would fall for me. I'm happy they are doing well; I've said they look really cute together. I was concerned that if they got together and even though she has two kids, he might want more but she would not be able to because of her recent emergency hysterectomy. Well I tell you, that little bitch was keeping a secret from me. She told me not to worry about it, that when she and Ben get married, she will just go to her doctor's office, retrieve her eggs and find a surrogate. I ask her how did she know about storing eggs and knew nothing about the whole sperm process and that bitch told me she wasn't interested in sperm she was only interested in storing her eggs. We both laugh and I tell her I'm happy for her and happy she was proactive to save for a raining day. She told me I should do the same. "Oh hell no, you don't have to worry about me storing shit," I say laughing. Nurse Jackie is back to keep an eye on the twins during the party. They are still small and we don't really want them to be exposed to too many people at once so we decide to keep them in the room and we will keep an eye on them as well. Our guests are starting to arrive. The detectives arrive bringing baby gifts and wine. The good Dr. Coverton arrives next then Ben and Coco. Other guests arrive within the next hour and then the moment we've all been waiting for, Justin. I am so happy to see my brother, I can't stand it! He hugs me hard and long; kisses me on the cheek and says, "I love you so much but I need to see my niece and nephew." I grab his hand and everyone is saying hello and hugging him on the way but he tells everyone he'll be back in a minute. We reach the twins' room and enter. Justin walks in and straight to their cribs. He looks in at Reign first and wipes away tears. He kisses his finger and places it on her forehead then does the same with River. He tells me they are the most beautiful babies he has ever seen. He confirms that he will always protect them and that nothing and no one will ever harm them. We turn to leave the room when I realize how rude I was by not introducing Nurse Jackie to Justin. "Justin this is Jackie, the twins' neo nurse." Justin reaches out to shake Jackie's hand but holds her hand a little longer, apparently making her a little uncomfortable.

"Don't I know you from somewhere? You look very familiar. Are you sure we haven't met? I generally don't forget a face," he says.

Chapter 27

Jackie tells me I'm mistaken and we have never met. I proceed to leave the room but look back at Jackie knowing I've seen her before and just can't put my finger on it right now but I will, because I never forget a face. Sydney and I rejoin the party and I make my way to the kitchen for a drink. It's bugging the hell out of me because I know that nurse and I need to find out from where. I'm going to try to enjoy my coming home party right now and I'll deal with that later. People are welcoming me home and I have no idea who half these people are but I respond with sincerity. I met Phoenix and his aunt for the first time. They seem pretty cool and my sister is digging this dude but I will still have to do my own research on this guy to make sure he is really on the up and up. The food is good and I'm so happy to be eating real food. I better take it slow because I've been eating shit for the past year and my stomach may not be able to handle it. When Kyle picked me up from the jail, we had a talk and he basically told me Amber went out on a limb for me and could be risking her profession and reputation if I don't do what I need to do to keep my nose clean. I tell him I get it and I appreciate everything that my sisters do and have done for me. I let him know that I have learned my lesson and I will not be seeing the inside of a jail ever again. My sisters hooked me up. Amber is letting me stay in her guesthouse. She set up all my sessions as part of my parole. I'm truly grateful for that because I was dreading making those calls. I would have made them but glad she did it. I knew Syd would hook me up with my clothes and she and Phoenix got my Convertible Ford Mustang out of storage. They had it detailed, washed and it

183

has a full tank of gas. I'll need to get my driver's license reinstated because when I went on 'vacation' it was suspended for a year. Did I say I was happy to be home? If not, well I am. I see a familiar face and make my way over to say hello. CoCo opens her arms to welcome me home. She tells me she missed me and was glad to see I kept myself looking good while I was away. We chat for a few minutes when I see someone I need to talk to. I've been trying to talk to this person since I got here but they have never been alone until now. "I'm surprised to see you here. I thought we were going to meet in a couple of weeks to discuss the latest events. I wasn't sure what you had in mind but from what I understand, it was brilliant. I believe this should make us even as far as favors are concerned and I'll no longer need your services since the task at hand is no longer a concern," I say. "Don't mention it. It was my pleasure to help in any way I could. It was a brilliant plan and I couldn't have carried it out more perfectly myself. Yes, this makes us even but if you ever need me, I'm here. Oh, by the way, there might be another issue on the rise, again if you need me, I got you," Dr. Brandon Coverton says. I look up and see Sydney looking right at us with a perplexed look on her face. Brandon notices the same thing and says, "She is a smart girl. I hope she doesn't put two and two together." I tell him, "that's why it's important that we're not seen together and if asked, I just met you tonight at the party." "Understood," Brandon says and walks away. The last thing I need is for Sydney to start suspecting something. We just need to let dead dogs lie and keep it moving. I continue to mingle and I look at CoCo and she still looks damn good. We used to mess around back in the day and I thought about hooking up with her when I got out but I see she's all up under this dude Ben so I won't cause any trouble. I'll leave her alone but sometimes I just like to fuck with people, you know stir the pot...or stir the pot (the sugar pot) if you know what I mean.

Don't get me wrong, I got the girls lined up and can have my pick of any and all of them but again I like to fuck with people. Auntie Hattie approaches me and asks if I'm having a good time. I tell her she outdid herself with the food as everything is off the chain. I tell her that I am about to pop because I have eaten so much. She laughs and tells me she's happy I'm enjoying myself and the food. I grab me another drink, take a seat and just people watch. Amber comes to check on me, asking if I am good and did I need anything. I tell her she is a good big sis and I'm happy to be home and in the presence of friends and family. She kisses me on the forehead and walks away. I see the nurse come out of the twins' room and head to the bathroom. I still can't put my finger on it but I'm one hundred percent sure I know her from somewhere. I get up from my seat and head to the twins' room. I'm standing over their beds admiring how beautiful they are and hope that one day I can find the right girl and settle down and have a family, then that thought quickly leaves as it comes because I got too much shit to do and the whole family thing is not in the program right now. I'll just have to live through my sisters right now until I do what I need to do. A few minutes later the door opens and the nurse comes back in. She has a nervous look on her face. "What's your name again?" I ask. "Jackie." "Where are you from Jackie?" "I grew up in Sacramento," she responds with hesitation. "How did my sister find you?" "They hired me from a registry and all my references check out," "So tell me Nurse Jackie, do you have any family here?" She tells me that she has a few cousins in Berkeley but that's about it. I ask her again is she sure we haven't met somewhere and that maybe it's possible we know some of the same people. She assures me that we have never met. She tells me she would remember a fine ass dude like me. Okay, she's flirting with me; I got this bitch right where I want her, I think. Not satisfied with her answer, I tell her, "Okay it was nice chatting with you Nurse Jackie and I want you to know that my sister and her fiancé are counting on you to take care of my niece and nephew. Should anything happen to either one of them under your watch, in fact if anything happens to them at all, I will hold you responsible and I will personally rip your heart out with my bare hands. Capeesh?" She swallows hard and nods in agreement. I walk out the room feeling like I got my point across. There's something about that bitch that's not sitting right with me and I don't want to bring it up to my sister because she has been through enough. I don't want to cause her anymore worry. So I'll do what I do best; take care of my sisters and now my niece and nephew and will take OUT anyone who tries to harm them.

Chapter 28

      The party was really nice. Everyone was happy to see Justin and the twins. Justin is so appreciative of the gesture. Phoenix and I open all the baby gifts we received and are grateful for all that we got but we really didn't need anything because we had already purchased everything we needed and wanted. We tell our guests who brought gifts that because we had all that we need, unless it was personalized; we ask their permission if we can donate the baby items to a shelter for battered women with newborns who don't have much of anything for their babies. That suggestion went over very well, in fact for those who didn't brings gifts, they offered to make a donation for the cause. I am so grateful that I cannot believe how generous people are. I now sit in front of the computer looking for a shelter to donate to since I didn't have one in mind. I just thought it would be a good idea and clearly it was. Once I found the right one that touches my heart, Phoenix and Ben load up the cars to drive the items to the shelter. Phoenix takes the cash and check donation and tripled the amount, providing the shelter with 10 thousand dollars. It's all about giving back he says. Shortly after they leave, Justin calls me to tell me he's coming over. I tell him great! I'll fix us something to eat once he gets here. He arrives about 15 minutes later and I admired how handsome my baby brother is and can completely understand why he's such a ladies' man. Anyway, he settles and sits at the kitchen table while I'm making some ham and cheese sandwiches. He asks me where is Nurse Jackie. I tell him she's in the nursery with the babies. He starts asking me all kind of questions about her and at first I thought he might be interested in her then I get the feeling he's not. I answer his questions and he seems to be satisfied but I think that it's weird he's asking. He tells me he's going to use the bathroom and I continue to prepare our little lunch.

I walk by the twins' room and hear Nurse Jackie on her cell phone. I gently crack the door open a little more and listen. "I'm not sure this is going to work. I want out. I didn't sign up for this shit. Her brother thinks he recognizes me from somewhere but I think I've convinced him that he doesn't. But get this, he threatened me and told me if anything happens to his niece or nephew he was personally going to rip my heart out with his bare hands and the look he had on his face told me he was telling the truth. He then smiled at me and walked out the door. I wanted to tell him, it's not your niece and nephew you should be worried about, it's that sister of yours. But I kept my mouth closed. He's got me scared as hell, which is why I want out. I don't want any parts of yawls plan anymore, the money ain't worth it." I gently close the door and continue to the bathroom. I get back to the kitchen where Sydney and Nurse Jackie are sitting at the table talking. "Well hello Nurse Jackie," I say. She damn near jumps out of her skin when she sees me standing there. Sydney observes how fidgety she is and how she's stumbling over her words. Sydney asks if she's okay. "Yes, Nurse Jackie, are you okay?" I ask. She looks at me and nods her head, tells my sister she's going to sit with the twins for a few more hours and if she doesn't mind, she'd like to leave a little early today. Sydney tells her that we are there all day and there's really no need for her to stay. Nurse Jackie excuses herself to get her belongings from the nursery and be on her way.

When she tells us goodbye, she hurries out the door. I tell Syd, "that girl is fine, Imma holla at her for a minute, be right back." I get up; exit the kitchen and then the front door. Nurse Jackie is standing in front of the elevator, waiting for its arrival. She hears the front door open and turns around to see it's me and clearly looks scared. I close the front door and walk so close to her that she can feel my breath on her face. I tell her, "You're sexy as hell. I like your lips and wonder how they will feel around my dick." She appears scared for a minute, and then says in a seductive voice, "Why don't you let me put them around your dick then." I smile and unbuckle my jeans to let them drop around my ankles. I move a little to the left so if my sister looks through the peephole, she won't see ole girl sucking my shit. She follows me and drops to her knees. Wow, she has skills. After she gets me off, she stands and says she needs to go. "Absolutely, but before you do, I need you to bend over and let me go up in that pussy." She hesitates for a quick second and says, "I don't have a condom." I step one foot out of my jeans, bend down to reach in my back pocket and pull out a Trojan Magnum. I hand it to her. She opens the wrapper, removes the rubber and places it on my still hard as steel dick. I turn her around and tell her to take off her scrub pants. She does as I ask. She bends over and looks back at me as to say, "I'm ready." Damn this chick must really be feeling me, cause she serving me this pussy on a silver platter. Or she must really be scared, either way she's about to get fucked. I go up in her with the quickness. Shit, I've been locked up for a year and ain't had none for a minute. Oh yeah, she's feeling me cause the pussy is nice and wet when I enter her. I don't know if she is really feeling the dick or if she just wants to be done because she's riding my shit like it's a mechanical bull. I slap her on the ass and tell her, "That's right, ride this dick." She cums and so do I. I pull out, take the rubber off and place it in the wrapper that's on the floor. I pull up my jeans and she pulls up her scrub pants. Nurse Jackie turns and looks at me but doesn't say a word. I push the elevator button to call the elevator to the 18th floor and before it comes I tell her, "I think I need to make myself a little more clear. You might have got the message regarding my niece and nephew so let me give you another message. If anything happens to my sister, not only will I rip your heart out, I will also slit your fucking throat. Actually, I'll cut your head off and your family will have to bury you without it. After your funeral service, I will mail your head to your mother. Do not fuck with my family. I will not say it again. The next conversation we have, you will be begging for your life. Do I make myself clear, Nurse Jackie? Thank you for the suck and fuck. I enjoyed it and that tight ass pussy, that shit was right." The elevator doors open, she rushes in and nods her head in agreement. "Have a blessed day," I say as the doors to the elevator close. I need to find out who the fuck she's working with. This is some type of set up shit. Well that bitch will damn sure go back to whoever she's working for and let them know she's out for sure. I probably should have waited to scare the shit out of her to find out who the ringleader of this little set up is. Looks like I got some extra cleaning up to do. I was hoping I could chill for a minute but it looks like there is no rest for the weary. I go back inside the apartment and call out for Sydney. "In the nursery," she responds. I walk in

190

the nursery and she's in the rocking chair feeding River. I turn to walk out to give her some privacy but she tells me to stay and that she's covered up. I still think it's a private moment and I should leave but she insists that I stay. I sit in the other rocking chair and admire how beautiful she is as a mother and how happy she looks. Reign begins to stir around. Sydney tells me to wash my hands, grab a bottle out of the fridge that she pumped this morning and to pop it in the microwave for 10 seconds to feed my niece. I was super excited and did as she told me. I walk back in the nursery and Reign is crying like someone is killing her. I tell her little cute ass to settle down, that uncle Jus is here. I hand the bottle to Sydney so she can test it and make sure that it's not too hot. She tells me it's perfect so I pick up my niece and sit in the adjacent rocking chair and gently place the nipple in her hollering mouth. She immediately latches on and starts sucking like she hasn't eaten in days. I stare at my niece and she stares at me. The love I have for these little people, words cannot explain. Even though I've always protected my sisters, I've killed for them and would do it again in a heartbeat, I make a decision right then and there that after I take care of this current situation, I will hang up my bad boy hat and try to fly right. That's hard to do when you got mutherfuckers coming for your family. At that point all bets are off. I will do what is necessary to protect them. Yeah they got husbands and boyfriends but they not hip to the game like I am so it's my responsibility to handle my business. I continue to hang out with my sister for several more hours. While she and the twins are napping, I take a trip to Phoenix's office to see if I can find any information on Nurse Jackie. I find her application,

191

referrals, and back ground and criminal history report. I see that she appears to be an upstanding citizen with no red flags on these reports.

Chapter 29

"So when did this bitch go bad and who the hell is she working for?" I ask myself. I take a picture of the information with my cell phone and made sure her address and phone number were clear because I see I have to pay the good nurse a visit. I place the papers in the rightful place and head back to the family room to put together my plan. I check in on the family and they're all still in la la land. I retrieve my cell phone to make a call. I tell the other person on the other end that we still got problems, however, the hit is for Sydney not the babies. I tell them that it doesn't matter who it is, the shit is not going down. "Whoever it is, they clever as fuck and the nurse is in on it as I walked in on her on the phone. I put the fear in her but I need to pay her a visit to find out who's behind this. I have a good idea who it is but I don't want to make any mistakes. I'm not in the business of fucking with people who ain't involved." I say. I continue to tell them that after my visit with the good nurse, I will have to put her ass to sleep just for even contemplating hurting my family. They agree and I disconnect the call. I sit, planning my next move and I have no time to waste because I'm sure Nurse Jackie has let her counterpart(s) know that I'm on to them. After Sydney's nap, we chat and ordered a pizza. When Phoenix got home, I left so that I can give them their privacy and I really didn't want to leave her home alone. I thought about telling Phoenix what I found out about Nurse Jackie but decided against it at the request of the person I spoke with earlier. They indicated that we should handle this ourselves and not to bring anyone else into this mess. Sydney and I are having a conversation a few days later and she mentions that Nurse Jackie has not shown up since the last time we saw her. She jokingly accuses me of scaring her off because I was flirting with her. She tells me that she and Phoenix have tried calling and texting her but to no avail. "I hope she's alright," she says. I tell her I'm sure she's okay and will respond or show up in a few days. She tells me that she and Phoenix were going to let her go shortly anyway because they were good with taking care of the babies. They were not having any issues and plus Auntie Hattie is available to help out if they need it anyway. I agreed with her decision and changed the subject.

The night I left Sydney's house after finding the information on Nurse Jackie in Phoenix's office, I drove to San Ramon to check out her place. She lives in a duplex on the bottom floor. The first night I drove by, I sat outside and watched movement inside the apartment. The curtains were somewhat see-through. I could see that two women were in there but could not make out who they were. I left and came back the next day. I did this for 3 days then on the 4th day, I waited until she left and 45 minutes after she left, making sure she didn't come back, I went up to the front door and tried to jimmy the lock. I was not able to do so because I didn't bring the right tools. I went around back and there was a cracked kitchen window. I also saw the upstairs neighbor leave as well so I knew the coast was clear. I needed to move quickly just in case somebody came back. Once inside the house, I walked slowly through the apartment. It was clean and nicely decorated. The colors were soft earth tones, I think they call them. Cream, brown, burgundy, and a mild green color was scattered throughout the apartment. Chairs, pillows, etc. It smells like a sage candle was being burned. If I didn't have to handle this chick, I'd have her decorate my place. I continue to walk through and I'm looking at the magazines she had on her coffee table, to the paintings she has on her walls. Then something interesting catches my eyes. I walk closer to a mantel to study the photos that sit perfectly on the shelf. I could not believe my eyes. I knew that bitch looked familiar! I just couldn't put my finger on it. Well it's all very clear. I leave out the same way I came in, got in my car and drive away. I hit the blue tooth in the car to make a call and once the caller answers, I fill them in on the most recent information I just found. We discuss how we are going to execute our plan and that if the opportunity presented itself, we would do it tonight. After ending the call, I make a trip to the nearest hardware store to pick up a few items. I park my car down the street, but can see the apartment clearly. I see my counterpart's car parked a few cars down the street in the opposite direction. I told them to wait for my text once I'm in and have the situation under control. Nurse Jackie pulls in her driveway about 9:46 p.m. She gathers the bags she has in the trunk and places them in front of her front door. She goes back to the car and retrieves her purse, hits the alarm on the car, and enters her apartment. I wait for about 30 minutes until I think she's settled in, and then I see the bathroom light come on, at the side of the house. I get out the car and inconspicuously walk to the side of the house to see if I can hear water running. I hear the water running and I can hear her singing. I think she's cute as hell but does not have the best shower voice. Anyway, while she's in the shower, I have the right tools to jimmy the lock and make my way through the front door. You can hear the music playing and her still singing. It appears that she's preparing for a date. The bags she took out of the trunk were Chinese food. She has the dining room table set for two and the cartons of food on the table. There are wine glasses and candles burning. Nurse Jackie must really love this person because she has gone all out preparing for this romantic evening. The food smells good and I open a carton and get lucky as the egg rolls are staring at me. I grab one and pop it in my mouth. I hear the shower water cut off so I make my way to the living room but before I do, I grab another egg roll. She's in the bathroom that's located near her bedroom so when she comes out the bedroom, I'll be sitting here chilling on her couch. Still singing, I guess she's getting dressed...or not. This set up looks like it's going down tonight with her boo. She finally leaves her room and walks right by the living room into the kitchen. She's wearing a hot pink lace camisole with a matching thong, stockings with garters and some 'come fuck me' pumps. She's bumping around in the kitchen when her house phone rings. She answers, singing her response to her caller. She tells them she is ready and will be waiting when they arrive. She also tells the caller that the front door will be open so just come on in when they get there. I hear a cork pop and her heels clicking on the kitchen floor, still singing and very happy. How is this bitch happy when she's involved in a plan to hurt someone? I guess I should ask myself that same question. Nurse Jackie walks in the dining room and says, "What the fuck? How did...?" she says but stops in mid-sentence. I can hear her thinking, then her heels coming in the direction of the living room.

Chapter 30

The sound of her heels is slowing as she enters the living room. When she sees me sitting on the couch, she drops the bottle of champagne she's holding and she covers her mouth to muffle her scream. "Come sit," I tell her and pat the seat next to me. Damn she looks good; I should have her suck my dick again. Poor little tink-tink, she looks terrified...she should be. Nurse Jackie sits next to me and begins to speak. "I'm sorry." I cut her off, put my finger up to her lips and tell her not to say a word. "What time will your date be here," I ask. She looks at me like she is asking for permission to speak. I tell her she can speak and she says, "Any minute." "Good, I can't wait to get this party started." I text my counterpart and provide an update on the situation. They are clear as to how to proceed. I grab Jackie's hand and lead her to the dining room. I tell her she just wasted a really good bottle of champagne. She asks if she should clean it up and I tell her no. "What I want you to do is to have a seat at this beautiful table you've prepared. I also need to know why you lied to me. I asked you several times haven't we met and you lied straight to my face and flat out lied. I probably would have taken it easy on you but there is nothing worse than a liar. What exactly did you and your other half, have planned for my sister?" I question. Nurse Jackie looks even more terrified at this point. Through clenched teeth, I ask her again because she didn't answer fast enough. Tears form in her eyes. I tell her, "there's no need for tears now sugar when just a week ago you were laughing about what was going to happen to my sister. Now tell me what the fuck was planned. Just as she was about to talk I hear the front door open and close. I put my finger up to my mouth letting her know she better not say a peep. "Babe? What happened? How did you drop the champagne?" With no answer, Keisha comes around the corner to find us sitting at the table. This shit talking, scary ass bitch turns to run out the door but is stopped by my counterpart who very quietly slipped in behind her. I look at Jackie and say, "Wow, did you see that? What kind of chick is she? She didn't even ask if you were okay, she just thought she'd make a run for it, save herself and fuck you. If I were you, I'd re-think my love and relationship with her, looks a little one-sided." I tell Keisha to sit her ass down at the table. She casually walks over and sits across from me. I move the dinner place setting so that it is front of her. I tell Jackie that the egg rolls are amazing and I apologize for eating most of them. I then tell Jackie to fix her and Keisha a plate. She looks at me like I'm crazy. "Fix the plates," I say. Jackie opens the cartons and places food on her and Keisha plates. "Why you fixen our plates," Keisha asks. "I hear Chinese is your favorite food, so why let it go to waste? This will be your last meal so at least it's your favorite food." Keisha stares at me like she's not fazed by my comment when I know she's shaking in her combat boots. "Listen here, enough of this bullshit. I'm just a little upset that your ignorant ass thought you could possibly try and hurt my sister and I not find out about it. You know me well enough Keisha to know I never forget a face but your dumb ass somehow gets my sister and her dude to hire your little girlfriend over here. Although she's a liar, she's not a very good one because her body language told it all. Nevertheless, she was just about to tell me how the two of you were going to carry out your little plan. But since you walked in, how about you do the honors?" "Fuck you," Keisha says. I tell them that I promised my sisters that I would never put my hands on another woman. I really meant that, however, this is a different situation. As little Scrappy from Love and Hip Hop Atlanta said, "Imma have to put them paws on you. I promise after you two, I will keep my promise to my sisters." Nurse Jackie is bawling out of control and she starts to beg for her life. She explains that Keisha put her up to it and planned the whole thing. She is about to say something else and Keisha tells her to shut her stupid ass up before she slaps the shit out of her. I look at Keisha and tell her if she so much lifts her fat ass off that chair, that I will put a bullet between her eyes. Again, she looks at me like she's not fazed. It's alright; I got something for her ass. Nurse Jackie is still crying out of control and this has gone on long enough. I'm trying to get this over with so I can get home to watch the second season of Scandal on Netflix. I motion for my counterpart who is just waiting for my word, to put our plan in motion. I have my counterpart tie Jackie's hands behind her back. They do as I say. I then take the materials that were placed on the table and walk over to Jackie. Keisha stands up like she's going to save her. I tell her to sit her ass back down. I take a tourniquet and begin to tie it around Jackie's arm and look for a vein. I tell her that I think she should go out just like Rocky did minus the shit dart. Well I don't think Jackie takes too well to my suggestion. She stands and even with her hands tied, her adrenaline kicks in and she puts up quite a fight. She's flipping around like a fish out of water. She falls and I pick her back up. When she's back on her feet, she tries to kick me with all of her might and loses her balance. She hits her head on the edge of the dining room table and knocks herself out. I bend down to see blood coming from the side of her head. I check for a pulse and low and behold, this damn girl has killed herself. "Great. This makes my job that much easier. Jackie did us a favor and we just need to take care of you," I say to Keisha.

I think that I have so much to live for. I've been given another chance to get it right. Well this shit didn't happen overnight so I'm sure I won't be 'fixed' overnight. I've been fucked up ever since I was 6 years old. In this situation I can have a clear conscience for the simple fact that yes, I came here to hurt/kill Jackie and Keisha. I thank goodness I didn't have to because Jackie took care of herself for me. I had no choice but to call in a favor to handle Rocky's punk ass. However, I wish I could have pumped that pure, one hundred percent uncut heroin into his veins myself. I'll have to tell you how that went down at a later date. Anyway, Sydney is happy with Phoenix and they are the best parents. She said they are going to start planning their wedding soon. Amber and Kyle selected their sperm donor and had their IVF procedure done. We all have our fingers crossed that she gets pregnant. Ben and CoCo seem to be happy with their little blended family; I still have plans to shake their little relationship up. Maybe I should try to settle down, find me a good woman who understands me. Well at least it's a good thought. I'm pulled from my thoughts when Keisha calls my name bringing me back. "Justin, please don't hurt me. You know we like family. I never wanted to hurt yo sis man, but she got my brother killed and I felt that's what I had to do. I was mad as hell and not thinking straight. I won't tell anyone what happened. Please just let me go," she says. I tell poor Keisha as good as that sounds, I can't leave any loose ends and unfortunately she's got to go. Keisha comes to realize that this is it. She pleads for her life to no avail. She screams out saying, "You know I got back-up. You know how many family members we got. They know that if anything happens to me to come looking for you. Yo family will neva be safe." "Yeah, yeah I know. I'll be ready whenever they get the balls to come for me," I respond. Realizing her words are falling on deaf ears, she's tries to make a run for it. She heads in the direction of the front door but trips over her own feet. She starts to crawl towards the door. I stand to end it for her once and for all, when my counterpart holds up a hand stopping me and letting me know they got her. I sit back down to watch our plan go down. Keisha now has so much fear in her eyes, that she stops fighting. Or so we thought. She gets close enough to the couch, which has a gun under it and quickly pulls it out. My counterpart sees what's about to go down and also pulls a gun from their side with a silencer on it. It appears with the quickness, I was very impressed and shocked at the same time. I thought to myself, "Handle your business." Within seconds, I hear a whistling sound and Keisha has a bullet hole in the middle of her forehead. "Wow, and a good shot. I'm really impressed. That shit was kind of sexy too. I didn't even know you had a gun. I guess if we have to go to battle, I know you got my back," I express. "Well, if you stay ready, you don't have to get ready. I didn't like that bitch anyway," Auntie Hattie says!

To be continued-

Check Out Other Smoking Hot Books From Bright Beginnings
Publications

A Taste of Honey

Sneak Attack

BRIGHT BEGINNINGS PUBLICATIONS

SOUTHERN CRIMES

PAMELA GULLEY

Made in the USA
Columbia, SC
08 June 2019